EllRay Jakes
is Magic!

EllRay Jakes
is Magic!

BY **Sally Warner**

ILLUSTRATED BY
Brian Biggs

VIKING

An Imprint of Penguin Group (USA)

VIKING

Published by the Penguin Group

Penguin Group (USA) LLC

375 Hudson Street

New York, New York 10014

USA ✦ Canada ✦ UK ✦ Ireland ✦ Australia ✦ New Zealand ✦ India ✦ South Africa ✦ China

penguin.com

A Penguin Random House Company

First published in the United States of America by Viking,
an imprint of Penguin Young Readers Group, 2014

Text copyright © 2014 by Sally Warner
Illustrations copyright © 2014 by Brian Biggs

LIBRARY OF CONGRESS CATALOGING-IN-PUBLICATION DATA

Warner, Sally, date.

EllRay Jakes is magic / by Sally Warner ; illustrated by Brian Biggs.

pages cm

Summary: Third-grader EllRay, a "shrimpy, goof-up kid," discovers magic all around him when he and his schoolmates participate in the Oak Glen Primary School talent show and work together on a wedding shower gift for their teacher.

ISBN 978-0-670-78500-1 (hardcover)

[1. Teachers—Fiction. 2. Talent shows—Fiction. 3. Schools—Fiction. 4. Magic tricks—Fiction. 5. Behavior—Fiction. 6. Family life—Fiction. 7. African Americans—Fiction.] I. Biggs, Brian, illustrator. II. Title.

PZ7.W24644Elw 2014   [Fic]—dc23   2013018236

Manufactured in China

1 3 5 7 9 10 8 6 4 2

Designed by Nancy Brennan   Set in ITC Century

To Dane Vincent Clark, of Boston, Massachusetts,

and

Austin Christopher Blevins, of Fall River, Wisconsin,

two of my favorite readers! —S.W.

• ▮ •

To Liam! —B.B.

CONTENTS

* * *

EllRay Jakes
is Magic!

🌟 1 🌟

KEEPING AN OPEN MIND

"Settle down, captive children," Ms. Sanchez says with a smile. It is after lunch on a Friday in April, but it feels like summer in here. Even though we're in a stuffy classroom, you can almost smell the chlorine in the air.

Our teacher's joke lately is to call us "captive children," because she knows we want to be outside playing, not stuck in our chairs like lumps of Play-Doh.

We take our seats in slow motion, not wanting to let go of the good time we just had during recess. All us third grade boys played hard, after cramming down our food as fast as we could. We played King of the Mountain, our latest fun thing, even though there aren't any mountains—or even pointy hills— on our playground. But there is a sloping lawn near where we eat lunch, so we make that work.

"Move it, swim boy," Jared Matthews says, hip-checking Corey Robinson for no reason.

Big mistake. Corey—one of my one-and-a-half best friends—ended up being King of the Mountain the longest today. He's quick. He's probably going to be an Olympic swimmer some day, which is pretty cool.

Corey turns around fast, and after some invisible, mysterious move, gigantic Jared is staggering backward. "Oops. Sorry, dude," Corey says, eyes wide and hands up to show his innocence.

And Jared doesn't say a word. In fact, I think he just learned something: to stay out of Corey's way.

My *half*-best friend is Kevin McKinley. He is the only boy in our class with brown skin like mine, but sometimes he hangs out with Jared and Stanley Washington now instead of Corey and me. That's new. It stinks.

The girls mostly huddled in the shade after lunch, because it was hot out. Girls don't like to sweat, in my opinion. They whisper and giggle and do whatever it is girls do when they're together. But Kry Rodriguez and Fiona McNulty joined in the game for a while, even though Fiona often claims she has weak ankles.

Kry can do whatever she wants, even boy stuff, and no one says anything bad about her. I don't know how she pulls that off, because a couple of girls in our third grade class—Cynthia Harbison and her personal assistant Heather Patton, to be exact—can be pretty strict about what is boy stuff and what is girl stuff. Kry has long, shiny black bangs that hang past her eyebrows in a perfect straight line, but she can still see.

Cynthia used to be the girl-boss of our class, but now I think Kry is, even though Kry doesn't act like she cares about stuff like that. I think Fiona was just copying Kry when she tried to play King of the Mountain with us, like maybe she thought some of Kry's popularity might rub off on her.

Emma McGraw and Annie Pat Masterson are the nicest girls in our third grade class, but don't tell them I said so. It might sound weird.

I think girls are confusing.

"It's time for you to listen," Ms. Sanchez tells us as we accept our fate and slump into our chairs. "I have an important announcement to make, and I want you to keep an open mind about it."

Keep an open mind about it? This does not sound good. When grown-ups say "Keep an open mind," they're usually about to tell you something you don't want to hear.

Besides, a couple of kids in our class—namely Jared and Stanley, the closest guys I have to enemies around here—already have minds that are so "open" they're almost empty, in my opinion. For example, Stanley says there's only one squirrel in Oak Glen, California, which is where we live. He swears that this lonely squirrel follows him around—and likes him. I think Stanley believes it because ever since he was three, his mom has said, "There's your little squirrel friend!" whenever they see one. I've heard her do it.

Meanwhile, back here in class, Heather raises her hand and speaks at the same time. "Well, whatever the announcement is, I'm not doing anything that's against my religion," she says, sliding a glance at the rest of us—especially Cynthia—to see how we are taking this news.

Since Heather has been yapping about it so

much lately, I happen to know that she and her family started going to a new church three weeks ago.

"Nobody would dream of asking you to," Ms. Sanchez says, her voice calm as always. "And please wait for me to call on you after you raise your hand. You know better than simply to blurt out whatever pops into your head, Miss Patton."

My name is EllRay Jakes, but I'm "Mr. Jakes" when I mess up in class. That's one of Ms. Sanchez's things, to get more polite the worse we act. But we usually don't act too bad, because we like Ms. Sanchez so much. Also, she's the prettiest teacher at Oak Glen Primary School.

And she's going to get married really soon! I feel funny thinking about it, but that sounds weird, too. All the parents are giving her a wedding shower late next week. They are arguing by email and phone-tree about what her present should be, and who owes what. I think they should just give Ms. Sanchez a sack of money. That's what I'd like if I were her.

My real name is Lancelot Raymond Jakes, but everyone calls me EllRay. My mom named me Lancelot Raymond because she writes romance stories for grown-up ladies, and she liked those two fancy names. But my name got changed to L-period-Ray for short, as soon as I got a vote, and then it turned into EllRay.

"So, here's what's up," Ms. Sanchez says. "Our principal has decided that Oak Glen Primary School should have its very own talent show next week, during Friday's assembly, which will be at two in the afternoon. He says that will help all the grades get to know each other better."

Emma raises her hand. "But it's already April," she says when Ms. Sanchez calls on her. "Why do we have to get to know each other better *now*?"

Annie Pat nods.

"I don't know," Ms. Sanchez says, sighing as she sneaks a peek at her sparkly engagement ring— which is her hobby, I think. "Maybe he thought that things were getting a little dull around here and you kids needed something fun to grab your attention. The point is, all grade levels have to take part in the show."

"I'm pretty sure talent shows *are* against my religion," Heather says, shaking her head like that's that, she's out of this thing free and clear.

"And we're going to need at least five volunteers from this very class for the talent show tryouts. *Five*," Ms. Sanchez continues, as if Heather hasn't said a word.

Okay. Keeping an open mind about this is gonna be *hard*.

"Corey can swim for everyone," Jared says, cracking himself up.

"Or Kry could do mental math," Kevin jokes—trying to impress Jared, I guess.

"And that's about it for talent in this class," Emma finishes, sounding sad.

"Oh, I don't know about that," Ms. Sanchez says, her brown eyes sparkling. "I'm sure some of you are taking music lessons or gymnastics. Or how about a martial arts demonstration? Anyone?"

We all **CLAMP** our mouths shut and shake our heads.

"Listen, people," Ms. Sanchez says. "Cheer up. It'll be fun! And the third grade has to participate. We can give it a try, at least. Remember, trying out doesn't mean you'll get in the show."

"Really?" Fiona peeps.

"Really," Ms. Sanchez says. "But I'll tell you

what. If you want, you may sort this out among yourselves. Just remember, we need five volunteers on Monday, because that's when the tryouts are.

"And now on to math and rounding money amounts," she announces, pulling some worksheets out of a bright green folder. "This is something you can *all* be good at, talented or not. Also, it's a useful, real-life skill to master. Let's proceed."

✻ **2** ✻

IN CHARGE

It is cloudy when we go outside for afternoon recess. It's like the day is the same as our new, gloomy mood, because there are invisible clouds over our heads. Both the boys and the girls in Ms. Sanchez's class huddle in the same group for once, near the picnic tables. At least the talent show has brought the boys and girls in the third grade together.

We *all* hate the idea.

"They're trying to make us look like fools," Jared says, scowling.

"Yeah," Kevin agrees. "In front of the big kids, too. Everyone will laugh at us."

"They'd better not laugh at *me*," Stanley says, looking as fierce as a kid can wearing a red plaid shirt and glasses.

Besides us and the little kids, there are fourth,

fifth, and sixth-graders here at Oak Glen Primary School. And some of the sixth grade boys are already shaving, I think. Not every day, but still. And some of the girls look like TV stars.

The thought of those big kids watching us, *laughing* at us, is terrible. Not to mention all the parents taking videos!

"I *know*," Cynthia says, agreeing with us boys for once. "It's not like we're in kindergarten or first grade. Kids in kindergarten look talented and cute just standing there *breathing*, but not us third-graders. We have to work at it."

"The kindergartners will probably hold hands and sing something," Heather says, shaking her head. "And everyone will say, '*Awww.*'"

"And then they'll clap like crazy," Kry adds.

"How could Ms. Sanchez do this to us?" Emma asks. "When she's going to get *married* soon?"

I don't see what getting married has to do with anything, but I speak up anyway. "We don't *have* to volunteer for the tryouts," I point out. "Maybe we can just say no."

"But the principal *said*," Annie Pat reminds

everyone. "And he's Ms. Sanchez's boss. And we told her we'd take care of it. We can't let her down. The third grade has to participate!"

It's weird to think of our teacher having a boss. She *is* the boss.

"I know a couple of fourth-graders who are good at stuff," Cynthia says, sounding gloomy. "This one girl can even tap dance. And fifth-graders are almost sixth-graders, so they're safe from being laughed at, no matter what. But not us."

"Who's talented in our class?" I ask, looking around. "Talented enough for the tryouts, I mean. Kevin?"

Hey, maybe he's developed some unknown skill since he's been hanging with Jared and Stanley so much!

"Huh?" Kevin asks. He has been peeling little pieces of dark green paint off a picnic table bench like that's his one and only job in life.

"What's your talent?" Corey asks him. Corey's probably sore about Kevin deserting us, too.

"Kevin can burp the alphabet now," Jared informs us.

"Only up to D," Kevin says, trying to sound modest.

"Except B, C, and D all kinda sound like the letter E," Stanley says, like he's only being honest. Not jealous.

"*Ew*, burping," a chorus of girls says, like they've been rehearsing it for days.

"Well, what can *you* do?" Kevin challenges them.

"Fiona's great at art," Cynthia announces, defending the girls' talent. "Especially drawing. And Heather can bend the tops of her fingers funny."

I'd like to see that!

Heather nudges Cynthia as hard as she dares and blushes. "I won't do it in front of an *audience*," she says.

"Anyway, those talents wouldn't show up very well from the back of our auditorium," I point out. "Five of us have to come up with something *big*, that shows up—but something we know won't make it past the tryouts. Because we don't want everyone making a joke out of us third-graders."

"Or the whole world making fun of us, if it goes

online," Corey reminds us all. "It could ruin our lives!"

Sometimes Corey gets carried away.

"I think it's just mean of Ms. Sanchez to make us do this," Cynthia says, pouting. "And we're working so hard to make her wedding shower all nice."

"With a fabulous present," Heather chimes in.

"If you call a toaster oven fabulous," Stanley says, shaking his head.

"That was ages ago. The toaster oven got voted down," Emma informs him. "I think that now, it's between one of those fancy vacuum cleaners and—"

"That's even worse," Jared interrupts, and for once I agree with him.

"So, let's just pick five people," I say, trying to get everyone back to the point.

My dad sometimes says that organizing people is "like herding cats," and I think this is what he means.

"Who made you king?" Jared asks, challenging me. "Ooo, I'm EllRay Jakes, and here's my crown,"

he says, plonking an invisible crown on his head. "**DOINK, DOINK, DOINK**."

"Ms. Sanchez said no more doinking," Emma tells him, hands on her hips.

I wish she wouldn't stick up for me!

"Look who's on your side, EllRay," Stanley says, pointing at Emma and laughing. "Your *girlfriend*."

"Yeah," Jared says. "*Smoochy, smoochy, smooch*," he says, giving big, slobbery kisses to the back of his hand.

"You can be nice to somebody without being their *girlfriend*," Annie Pat says, turning pink—which is what happens when she gets mad, I have noticed. Maybe it's because she has red hair. "And EllRay's right," she continues. "We should just get this over with now, and pick five people to try out—and **FAIL**. Then we can tell Ms. Sanchez who they are, first thing on Monday."

"Wait," I tell them. "Let's think about it over the weekend, okay? Because we have to make it look real, remember. Like we're actually going along with this. Or else she'll get upset before she gets married, and that's not good."

"Yeah," Corey says. "EllRay's right. Getting married is hard enough. So everyone come up with one talent that sounds real over the weekend, and we can meet up and choose who has to try out before school starts on Monday."

"Or else we can be absent that day," Fiona says, probably thinking aloud.

"No fair, Fiona," I tell her. "Even girls with weak ankles can be talented at *something*. And if you're not here, we'll nominate you for the tryouts for sure. We'll say you want to—to *juggle* for the tryouts. Juggle raw eggs! And then you'll have to do it! And clean up afterward, too."

"Cool," Stanley says, laughing.

"That's just mean," Fiona says, tears springing into her eyes—which *is* one of her talents, come to think of it. But, like doing good art or bending your fingers funny, crying wouldn't show up very well in our auditorium.

Which, remember, will be full of possibly whiskery sixth grade boys.

I am the shortest kid in our class, by the way, and I look *TINY* next to those guys. My dad keeps promising that I'll grow, but *when*?

"So show up," I tell Fiona. "And everyone think of some fake talent you can do. Then five people can sacrifice themselves for the tryouts—but not the talent show, don't worry—before school starts Monday morning."

"Are we gonna draw names out of a hat?" Corey asks, his brow wrinkling. He's kind of a stressball sometimes, but like I said, he's cool. And he's my best friend. He has three hundred freckles, he told me once.

"If we have to," I say. "At least that way we'll be

the ones in charge. That's the important thing."

"If you say so, EllRay," Corey says, trying to be loyal.

"*Doink, doink, doink*," Jared whispers again, fiddling with his—*my*—invisible crown.

"You got a better idea?" I challenge him.

"I guess not," Jared admits, shrugging.

"Then put on your thinking cap this weekend," I say as the buzzer sounds, using one of Ms. Sanchez's favorite expressions. "If you even have one, that is."

"Excellent," Corey murmurs, low-fiving me as we head for class like those little iron filings being pulled by a magnet, which we did in Science Activities once. I forget why.

We're the iron filings in this comparison, and Ms. Sanchez's class is the magnet.

But this time, the iron filings are going to be in charge—for once.

✻ **3** ✻

MY ONE AND ONLY SISTER

Alfie and I get up early on Saturday mornings and eat cereal in front of the TV while Mom and Dad sleep late. We take turns choosing DVDs or TV shows. Today it is Alfie's Saturday to choose, which is why we are watching *Pink Princess Fairies*. I'm just glad Jared and Stanley can't see me now. I would never live this down.

Alfie frowns. "I think I saw this one before," she says, pointing at the TV screen with her dripping spoon.

"How can you tell? They're all the same," I say, after slurping down the last of my cereal milk from the bowl.

"They're *not* all the same," Alfie argues, scowling.

"Sure they are," I say. "The littlest pink princess fairy always gets into trouble, and the bigger ones save her. And that baby dragon always shows up, too."

"But it's different *kinds* of twouble," Alfie points out. "And the fairies wear different outfits every time."

"But they're always pink and sparkly outfits," I say.

"Or else they wouldn't be *pink princess fairies*," she explains. "Duh!"

Alfie is four years old, and she is my one and only sister. Her real first name is Alfleta. That is

the Old Saxon word for "beautiful elf." Why Old Saxon, which my father told me hasn't been spoken in more than a thousand years? It's because of my mom and those romantic books she writes. And when Alfie was born—I was four years old—Mom said that was her new baby girl's name, period.

I think a lady who has just had a baby gets the biggest vote on what to name it, so my dad didn't argue.

And Alfie *did* look like a golden brown elf. She still does, a little. She's really cute, but I don't tell her that very often. She's bad enough. Besides, my mom says girls shouldn't only get praised for being cute.

"Anyway," Alfie says, as if that's what we've been talking about all along, "I'm going out with you and Dad this morning when you do your chores."

"You're not," I say, keeping my voice matter-of-fact and calm, which usually works with her. "You and Mom do girl chores on Saturdays, and me and Dad do—"

"You have to let me come with you and Daddy, EllWay, or it's against the law," Alfie says. "You can't gang up against girls. Suzette Monahan says so."

Suzette Monahan is one of Alfie's best friends and worst enemies at Kreative Learning and Playtime Daycare. And yes, I know they spelled "creative" wrong.

Suzette is what my mom calls "a real handful."

"Nobody is ganging up on anyone around here," I tell my sister, stacking our cereal bowls. "You and Mom do fun girl stuff on Saturdays, and Dad and I do . . ."

I don't finish my sentence, because I can't exactly claim that what Dad and I do on Saturday mornings is **FUN**. We do not have a lot in common. My dad is a college professor and a geology scientist, see, and his brain is usually busy thinking about stuff like radio isotopes, which he says tell us how old rocks are. And I'm just an eight-year-old kid. I think about my two favorite basketball teams, the Lakers and the Clippers, and scoring snacks, and funny videos starring cats and dogs. We can't have a pet because Alfie's allergic.

We try to have fun, though. And I like hanging out with Dad. I kind of spy on him, in fact—but not in a creepy way—to see how a man does things.

My dad never loses stuff, for example. I'm exactly the opposite.

But even a brainy geology scientist has other things to do. We almost always do three errands and then have one secret Saturday treat. We usually go to the hardware store, because my dad likes to fix stuff, and the plant nursery, because he grows roses, and then we go to a yard sale or two. My dad says you never know when someone's going to toss out some interesting rocks or crystals.

Once, Dad even found a little meteorite mixed in with a bunch of marbles and stuff in a shoe box lid on a card table! That was cool, because meteorites are pretty rare. The meteorite Dad found was the size of a peanut. It looked like a twisted piece of rusty metal. But instead, it was basically a visitor from outer space, Dad said. Only luckily, not the **DROOLLY** kind with fangs you see in scary movies I sort of like.

See, my dad told me once that a meteorite is a natural object that falls to earth from outer space, which is enough all by itself to make a person nervous. I'm never telling stressball Corey about rusty peanut-shaped meteorites falling from outer space, that's for sure!

Meteorites can either be "falls" or "finds," my dad says. A "fall" is a meteor you actually see falling from the sky, and they are pretty rare—which is good or else you might get bashed when it comes down. A "find" is a meteorite that came down sometime in the past, maybe hundreds of years ago. Or thousands.

Or yesterday, if you live in Siberia, even though Dad says it's just a coincidence that so many land there.

The secret treat my dad and I get every Saturday is one doughnut each, which is the reason Alfie can't come with us. She could not keep quiet about eating a doughnut for more than a minute, tops, and my mom's really into healthy foods.

Well, my dad and I are too, officially. But this is only once a week. It's a guy thing we do together, and I want to keep it that way.

I go out alone with Mom sometimes, too, usually to lunch or to a movie that she doesn't want Alfie to see. And Alfie sometimes goes out with Dad. She gets all dressed up, too. You should see her.

"You and Dad eat cookies when you go out," Alfie says like she's accusing me, *Pink Princess Fairies* forgotten for the moment. "There was chocolate on your shirt when you came home last week, EllWay."

My sister the master detective!

My sister the chocolate hound is more like it. Chocolate is Alfie's favorite food group.

"Okay, maybe we had *a cookie*," I fib, pretending to admit it. "One cookie, Alfie, with chocolate on top. But if we ever do it again, I'll bring one home for you."

"Me and Mom have to go to the farmer's market," Alfie says with a pout, not giving it up. "And all I get is fwee samples of fwoot."

That's "free samples of fruit," in Alfie-speak.

"Listen, Alfie," I tell my little sister. "I promise I'll bring home something good for you today, okay? From one of Dad's yard sales?"

"But not a rock," Alfie warns me.

"Not a rock."

"Something chocolate?" Alfie asks, hope making her shiny brown eyes look even bigger than they already do.

"Or even something *Barbie*," I promise. "Or some jewels."

Alfie is big into used jewelry these days, the junkier and shinier the better. She likes to glue it on stuff. My mom says she's being creative.

"You won't forget?" she asks.

"Nuh-uh," I say, getting ready to bail on *Pink Princess Fairies* once and for all.

There's usually a tangle of messed-up jewelry somewhere at a yard sale.

"Then okay," Alfie says. "And I'll bwing you fwoot."

"Deal," I tell her, and we shake hands on it.

✱ 4 ✱

"YOUR AMAZING FIRST MAGIC SET, WITH TOP HAT, WAND, AND DVD!"

"We'd better go, or Alfie's gonna have a meltdown," I warn Dad as he studies his list of chores in the driveway, even though I don't see why he needs a list. Like I said, we pretty much always do the same thing.

"That's 'going to,' not 'gonna,' son," my dad says. "No lazy tongues at our house, please."

But he **BIPS** open the car door locks, and we get in and buckle up.

"I was checking a few addresses for a sensible driving plan," Dad tells me as he backs out of our driveway. "Because I thought we'd hit the yard sales first, for a change."

"What are you looking for?" I ask as Dad heads away from where most of the houses are in Oak Glen.

"Just the usual," Dad replies.

Oak Glen is about halfway between San Diego and Disneyland. I'm not sure why they built a town here in the first place, now that I think about it. But, like just about every place in California, my dad says, it's getting bigger every year.

Our town is partway up a low mountain. It curves around a couple of bulging, rocky foothills like it's a stretched-out cat taking a nap in some giant's garden.

If Oak Glen *were* a sleeping, stretched-out cat, Oak Glen Primary School would be sitting on the cat's head, our house would be on its chest, and we would be driving around one of the almost treeless hills toward the pretend-cat's tail.

"What about you?" Dad asks, like he just reminded himself to be polite and ask me questions, too. "Looking for anything special today?"

"Just a present for Alfie," I say. "You know, a broken bracelet, or something else sparkly. Or maybe some old Barbie stuff. Um, Dad?" I ask.

"Mmm?"

"Were you or Mom talented when you were kids?"

"Talented like how?" Dad asks, his forehead wrinkling as he thinks back. "I learned my times tables before anyone else in class. Felt pretty darn good about it, too," he says, smiling a little.

Wow, *that* skill sure didn't get passed down. Not to me, anyway.

Not with seven-times-*anything*—except one or ten.

But I try to imagine standing in front of the Oak Glen Primary School Talent Show Tryout Committee, stumbling over my times tables. Would that satisfy Ms. Sanchez and our principal?

"You weren't talented at music or anything?" I ask, my voice hopeful.

"Sorry," Dad says, shaking his head. He turns off onto a smaller road.

He signals even when there are no other cars around, I have noticed.

"What about Mom?" I ask, still hopeful. Maybe there's still some hidden family talent that was passed down to me—only I don't know it yet.

"Hmm," Dad says. "She likes to sing."

Okay. I may only be eight years old, but *already*

I know that "liking to sing" isn't the same as being able to sing. Sing *well*, that is.

I mean, I like my mom's lullabies and random kitchen, garden, and shower songs fine, but she's not exactly *talented*. No offense.

"What other talents are there in life?" I ask my dad.

"Why this sudden interest in talent, EllRay?" Dad says, slowing as we approach a line of cars parked along the edge of this dusty road.

"It's for school," I say, shrugging. "See, our principal got this idea that the whole school should have a talent show at assembly next week. Ms. Sanchez just announced it yesterday."

"Really?" Dad asks, pulling in behind an out-of-state SUV. "That seems kind of last-minute, doesn't it? The school year's over in a couple of months."

"I *know*," I say, agreeing with him. "It's messed-up, right? And the whole thing's so embarrassing! It's going to end up just being talented fifth- and sixth-graders, *obviously*, because they're the only ones who are good at stuff. Or at least the only ones nobody will boo off the stage. And maybe they'll throw in a few kindergarten kids, for laughs."

"So what's the problem?" Dad asks. "That sounds like a show."

"It's the principal," I try to explain. "He told Ms. Sanchez that every class has to take part—in the tryouts, anyway. So Ms. Sanchez says that our class has to come up with at least five tryout acts. We have until Monday morning."

"Maybe there's some hidden talent in your class you don't know about," Dad says as we cross the empty road—after looking both ways, of course.

"Dad, *please*. You know my class," I say, eyeing the groups of yard sale shoppers—the competition—clustered around the card tables and blankets scattered across the yard sale family's dried-up lawn. I look for the jewelry-tangle table and the kids' area.

"Point taken," Dad says, laughing. "Although some of the girls in your class might surprise you, EllRay. They're probably taking lessons in all kinds of things." He sighs.

"That's what Ms. Sanchez said," I tell him. What is it with girls and talent? Alfie's already nagging Mom and Dad for classes in ballet, horse riding, gymnastics, and *archery*, which is just one **SCARY** idea.

"Maybe," I say. "But none of them stepped up when we were talking about it on Friday, that's for sure."

"Too bad," Dad says, heading like an arrow for a table with an old basket of geodes on it.

He doesn't seem too worried about my problem.

But that's okay, I figure—because I'm worried enough for both of us.

I spot it five minutes later, among a bunch of other toys spread out on an old picnic blanket on the brown grass. The toys include:

1. A marionette cowboy puppet whose strings are so badly tangled that the puppet looks permanently frozen in place, like something from a monster movie. Not that I've ever seen a cowboy puppet in a monster movie.

2. A handful of little metal cars that look as if they were left out in the rain—for a year or two.

3. A bucket full of small plastic building blocks that

look like someone spilled pancake batter on them a long time ago.

4. And, most important and best of all, a colorful but faded cardboard box that is taped shut and labeled "Your Amazing First Magic Set, with Top Hat, Wand, and DVD!"

There's a five dollar sticker on the box.

Magic. That's it! Magic is a talent, isn't it?

"It's missing the DVD," the bored-looking teenage kid guarding the blanket tells me. "And I think the top hat got wrecked, so that's gone, too. But otherwise it's good. You should get it, bro."

I have only three dollars in my pocket, and I wanted to spend at least a dollar to buy a present—okay, a *bribe*—for Alfie. And he's not my "bro."

But even if I spent all my money on myself, I wouldn't know how to turn three dollars into five dollars. I'm not that good a magician—*yet*.

My dad says you can usually bargain with the sellers at yard sales, but I don't know how to bargain—especially with a teenager.

I don't even know whether I should try to look rich or poor.

So I just stand there, as frozen as the tangled

cowboy puppet, staring at the taped-shut magic set. "Does it still have the wand?" a voice behind me asks.

Dad! Just in time.

"Yeah," the boy says, standing up a little straighter. "And a few props. I *think*."

"What about an instruction booklet?" Dad asks.

"Most of the instructions were on the DVD, which got lost," the teenager says, scowling. It sounds like he's blaming the DVD itself for getting lost.

So basically, he's trying to sell a box with a stick—excuse me, a *wand*—inside it.

"How about three dollars?" the kid says, starting to sound desperate.

"Can you afford three dollars?" Dad asks me.

"I can afford two dollars," I tell him. "Because I have to save a dollar for Alfie's present. I promised."

"Hey," the kid says, eager for a sale. "If you're gonna spend money on something else here, too, I'll let you have this magic set for two dollars. It's really cool," he adds, not sounding very convincing.

"Did you learn any tricks?" Dad asks him.

Besides figuring out how to sell a taped-shut box with a stick in it for two dollars, I guess Dad means.

"I could kind of make something small disappear," the teenager says, trying to remember. "But that was a few years ago. Do you wanna look inside the box?" he asks.

I can tell he's scared we'll say "Yes."

"EllRay?" Dad asks. "You're the buyer, son."

"No. That's okay," I tell the kid. "Here's your two dollars," I add, fishing the **CRUMPLED** bills out of my pocket.

"You're sure you don't want to look inside the box?" Dad asks me. "'Let the buyer beware,'" he adds, quoting from somewhere.

My dad loves quotations. I think that's part of being a college professor.

"I'm sure," I tell him, tucking the almost-empty box under my arm. We walk away from the toy blanket and the relieved teenager. "Because it's perfect, see?" I tell Dad. "For the talent show!"

"The lamer the better," is what I don't add. It's my own *silent* quotation.

Because—I don't want to get *in* the talent show, remember?

I just have to try out and get it over with so we don't let Ms. Sanchez down.

And that's worth two dollars any day of the week.

✷ 5 ✷

DOOMED

"I thought you said Sundays were meant for hikes and picnics," Alfie says, sitting inside a circle of dolls and doll clothes. She looks like an angry cartoon kitten when she's mad, I sometimes think.

"It's raining out," Dad says, not looking up from the newspaper.

Yes, we still get actual newspapers at our house.

"It's not real rain," Alfie argues, staring out the window.

"You're right, honeybun," Mom says, giving her a hug. "It's more like a drizzle, really. It's still wet out, though."

"But I wanted to bring my sparkly lunch box with us," Alfie says. I can hear the wobble in her voice from where I am sitting cross-legged on the family room rug. I have been going through my not-so-amazing first magic set with no top hat, the lamest wand in the world, and no DVD for probably the tenth time.

That wobble in her voice means Alfie's clouding up, which means she's about to **BURST** out crying. And her bad moods can last forever.

But I'll leave that problem to my mom.

"I know what," Mom says, sounding both desperate and inspired. "I'll make a special indoors picnic, and you can show us your sparkly lunch box then. And I promise we'll all be amazed. How does that sound?"

The "sparkly lunch box" Alfie is talking about has all those fake jewels on it. First, my dad spray-painted an old lunch box gold for Alfie. Since then, Mom has been helping her glue stuff onto it: pieces of the broken-down jewelry we've found at yard sales, sequins, and fake diamonds and rubies from the craft store. Mom has to use special grown-up glue for most of the stuff, but Alfie gets to paste down the sequins all by herself.

She usually ends up with one or two of them stuck to her, somewhere.

"Oka-a-y," Alfie says, sounding sorry to give up her gripe so soon. And Mom goes into the kitchen to make our pretend picnic.

I move my magic set supplies around on the rug as if that might make them look different, better. But here's what was in the taped-shut box:

1. One wand, as promised. It's really a hollow black cardboard tube with a silver paper band at each end, though. I guess you're supposed to be able to pull a silky scarf or something out of the tube, only sorry, no scarf was included.

2. One big plastic coin that my dad says looks like a poker chip.

3. One pretend egg. *Buk, buk, buk.*

4. One bunny hand puppet. Alfie snagged it right away, so it's not really in front of me now. But I didn't know what to do with it anyway, so I don't care.

5. One dead spider crumpled up in a corner of the box. I guess it gave up on ever becoming a magician and astounding all its spider friends.

"How's it going over there, EllRay?" my dad asks, glancing over the top of his newspaper.

"Terrible," I admit. "You can't tell by looking at any of this stuff what you're supposed to do with it. Anyway, I don't think there's enough here to do even a *bad* trick for the talent show tryout, not that magicians call them 'tricks.' You're supposed to call them 'effects' or 'illusions,' the box says. But I'm doomed without that DVD."

"What talent show?" Alfie asks, looking up from her dolls.

"They're making us have one at our school assembly next week," I tell her. "All the grades have to try out, but I'm pretty sure it'll just be the big kids who get chosen."

"Can I be in it?" Alfie asks.

"No, Alfie," Dad says, answering for me. "You don't go to Oak Glen Primary School yet, remember? That pleasure still awaits you."

Dad talks fancy like that, sometimes.

"I saw a talent show on *Pink Princess Fairies* once," Alfie says, not giving up. "And the baby dragon danced in it and won. I can dance as good as that."

Alfie *thinks* she can dance.

"You dance as good as a dragon?" I ask, teasing.

"As *well* as a dragon," Dad corrects me, not even hearing how goofy that sentence sounds.

"Okay, Alfie can dance as well as a dragon," I say. "But *no*, Alfie. You cannot try out for our talent show. I'm sure there will be another one when you go to Oak Glen. But maybe you should start practicing now."

"Maybe you should be quiet, *EllWay*," Alfie tells me.

She does not like being teased.

"That's enough," Dad says in his quiet, but *I-MEAN-IT* voice.

"He started it," Alfie mumbles as the rain starts to come down so hard outside that you can hear it pattering on the roof upstairs.

"Enough," Dad says again, a little louder this time. "And EllRay, I don't think you're doomed at all, DVD or no DVD. You've got a much better resource than that handy. A great resource."

"What resource?" I ask.

"The Internet, son," Dad says. "Specifically, You-Tube. I'm always looking up how to fix things on YouTube. People like nothing better than to teach other people how to do things, so they're always putting up posts. How do you think I fixed the toilet last weekend?"

I don't even want to *imagine*. I never knew it was broken!

"But magicians wouldn't explain any of their

illusions on YouTube," I say, afraid to get my hopes up. "Isn't there some rule about magicians never giving away their secrets?"

"They're not going to show you something stupendous, like how to make a motorcycle disappear," Dad says. "But I'm sure you'll be able to find some simple tricks—excuse me, *illusions*—that will be good enough to get you through the tryouts. And maybe even into the talent show."

Ohhh, no. What I'm looking for is something a little less good than that, I tell myself, hiding my losing smile.

"Let's go into my office and take a look on the big computer before our picnic is ready. That way, we can study the details of the illusions you like best," Dad says, his eyes lighting up. He loves a project.

And it's "we" now, I notice.

Well, that's fine with me, I tell myself as we head for Dad's home office, Alfie trailing close behind us.

Let him do the work!

✳ **6** ✳

TA-DA!

We go back to my dad's computer after our picnic lunch in the family room, where Alfie stunned us with her jewel-covered lunch box—which is now so heavy she can hardly lift it. Dad has found some cool posts that show a guy demonstrating simple illusions.

"We're narrowing it down," he says.

"Why don't we just get in the car and go to Target or someplace and buy a better magic kit?" I ask.

"First, it's pouring out," Dad says, nodding toward the rain-spattered window, "and second, you don't see this magician using a store-bought magic kit, do you?" he asks, pointing at the computer screen. "He's using everyday objects we already have around the house."

"But I can't learn a bunch of magic before tomorrow morning," I say, trying not to sound too whiny. Because I don't want the lecture on *that*.

"You don't have to learn 'a bunch of magic,' as you put it," Dad says. "Just enough for the tryouts. Maybe two tricks, EllRay. *Illusions*, I mean. It's mostly a matter of practice, this man says."

"So I'm supposed to stay up all night practicing?" I ask. "And—which two tricks? They all look pretty hard to me! Even after he explains them."

"That's what makes them good," Dad says. "They're easy, with practice, but they *look* difficult. And I think I know just the ones you should try."

"Which ones?" I ask.

"The illusions he calls 'Making Money' and 'Cut String Made Whole,'" Dad says, checking his notes. "We can start on those right now, and you can practice like crazy. Then you can try them out on Alfie and Mom and me after dinner."

"I think it's too late for 'Making Money,' Dad," I say, thinking of the dollar bills I handed over to the teenager at the yard sale—for a magic set I can't even use.

He's probably laughing his head off right now, or rolling around on my dollar bills.

"It's not," Dad tells me. "Let's watch that one

again, and then the cut string one. I'll get your supplies ready after that, and you can start practicing."

I only want to practice enough to try out and *not get in* the talent show, but of course I don't explain this to Dad. It would definitely sound like "having a bad attitude," which is something that is frowned upon around here.

So I sit and stare at the computer screen, hoping I don't fall asleep.

"And now, ladies and—and little lady," Dad says at the dining table, after the dinner dishes have been cleared, "I present EllRay the Amazing!"

"Huh. The amazing what?" Alfie says to Mom.

She's jealous, and I haven't even done anything yet!

Mom, Dad, and Alfie are sitting at one end of the table, and I am standing opposite them. I have one of my dad's goofy old hats on my head to make me look more magical, since I don't have that top hat. My heart is actually **POUNDING**, and this is just my family. Imagine me doing these two tricks in front of my class—or the Oak Glen Primary School Talent Show Tryout Committee!

I'd probably collapse.

"EllRay the amazing *magician*, Alfie," Dad tells her in his best settle-down voice. "Now, prepare to be astonished, one and all. Announce your first illusion, son."

I can tell Alfie really wants to ask Mom what "illusion" means, so I answer my little sister's question before she can ask it. "'Illusion' is another word for a magic trick," I begin in a boomy voice that sounds only a little like mine. "And tonight, I will perform two illusions just for you."

Talking is an important part of doing magic, I learned from the guy on YouTube. That and waving your hands around a lot—if you can do it without messing up your illusion.

First, though, I fiddle my fingers under the table, preparing illusion number one, "Making Money." The preparation is the hardest part of this trick, I have learned.

There, ready.

"I show you this ordinary dime. Or is it so ordinary?" I say to Mom, Dad, and Alfie. I hold the dime directly facing them, between my thumb and middle finger, so that's the only thing they can see. But *behind* the dime are two quarters, held standing up and sideways by the same two fingers. The dime hides them, kind of forming the top part of the letter T.

"So what? I have a dime," Alfie mutters.

"But **ABRACADABRA**," I say, passing my other hand in front of the dime—just long enough to push the dime behind one of the quarters with my thumb. I pinch the quarter with the dime behind it together, hold the coins up, and hold up the other quarter with my other hand. "Ta-da!" I say, displaying the two quarters.

They can't see the dime at all.

At the other end of the table, Dad is grinning. He gives me a secret thumbs-up. All that practicing paid off! At first, I kept dropping the quarters. My fingers are pretty small.

Mom looks surprised, and then she starts clapping.

But Alfie looks truly astounded. She jumps up and charges over to me the way Dad said she would—which gives me just enough time to hide the dime in the palm of my hand. "Let me see those," Alfie says, and she takes the quarters from me and turns them over and over on the table, as if that will somehow reveal how I did it.

"It's magic, Alfie," I say.

"Then why aren't you rich, if you can make quarters out of dimes?" she asks.

"Come on back here and sit down, love," Mom says to her. "EllRay the Amazing has one more trick to perform, I think."

"Illusion," Dad whispers to her.

"Illusion," Mom says.

And Alfie trudges back to her seat.

✳ 7 ✳

FAMOUS ALL OVER THE WORLD

I clear my throat, getting my magician voice ready again. "And now," I say, "I will show you the 'Cut String Made Whole' illusion, famous all over the world."

I made up that last part all by myself.

"I can cut a *stwing*," Alfie says, refusing to be further astonished. I think she's confused enough about how I made those quarters appear out of nowhere.

"First," I tell my audience, "I take a plain drinking straw and push a length of ordinary string all the way through it, until the string pokes out the other end."

And I do it.

The string just has to be longer than the straw, that's all. Dad prepared a whole bunch of straws for me. Using an X-Acto knife, which has a pointy razor blade at the end, which is why a grown-up needs to do it, he cut long, invisible slits down the middle parts of the straws, but only on one side. Not all the way through.

"See?" I say, holding up the drinking straw with string hanging out both ends.

"So what?" Alfie says, and Dad gives her a look.

"Now," I tell them, "I will bend the straw in half, like *so*."

I bend the straw in the middle, slit side facing

down. I hold the two straw ends together in one hand, partway down from the top, tugging the loose string ends straighter. As I do this, I am really pulling the looped string down about an inch through the slit in the straw. I hide the pulled-down loop of string with the fingers holding the straw, so nobody can see it.

"Now, I am going to cut this straw in half," I say, waving the kitchen scissors around in a magical way with my other hand.

And I snip off the top, bent piece of the straw.

"There goes the poor little stwing," Alfie predicts in a gloomy voice.

"And *abracadabra*, the cut string is whole again! Ta-da!" I say, letting the two straw pieces fall to the table.

I wave the entire uncut length of string back and forth in the air.

It worked!

Mom and Dad clap their hands and cheer, but Alfie's eyes are wide.

She's actually **SCARED**!

"Want to see the string, Alfie?" I ask, holding it out to her. "It's just regular string. Don't be afraid."

"No-o-o," she cries, burying her face against Mom's sweater. "Get it away fwom me!"

"It's okay, Alfie. You don't have to touch it," I say, trying to calm her down.

"Honey! What on earth's the matter?" Mom asks, squeezing Alfie tight.

"*EllWay is magic*," Alfie wails so loud that the neighbors can probably hear. "He's magic! Don't let him touch me and cut me in half, or turn me into two quarters!"

My sister the drama queen. Or drama *princess*, I guess. She's only four.

"No, Alfie," Mom says. "It was only a trick, darling. EllRay's not magic. He's learning to be a *magician*. There's a big difference."

"Not to *me-e-e*," Alfie says, sniffling big time, and Mom holds her away a little before her small nose gets wiped on Mom's pretty blue sweater, which is almost new.

"Time for somebody's bath, story, and bedtime," my dad says, getting to his feet and lifting Alfie—who is now kicking—from my mom's arms. "Because somebody's *tired*."

"Wah-h-h!" Alfie cries as Dad takes her from the dining room.

"Wah-h-h!" I hear her voice fade as he carries her upstairs.

And I'm left standing there with a long piece of string in my hand. I should figure out a better way to finish, I guess.

"Don't pay any attention to your little sister, darling," Mom tells me. "Those were wonderful illusions. Ms. Sanchez is going to be *thrilled.*"

Oh, yeah, I think, startled. The tryouts! I was so busy trying to learn those two tricks all afternoon—and having fun—that I forgot I was supposed to stink at them.

Well, there's still time for that.

✳ **8** ✳

OUR CLASS'S FIVE LAME ACTS

The kids in my class agreed to meet Monday before school starts, to plan the tryouts for the talent show. I'm the first one at the sloping lawn near the picnic tables. That King of the Mountain game we played here seems like it happened a long time ago, even though it was just last Friday. Those were the days.

I have decided not to volunteer first for the tryouts—even though I brought all my stuff.

Doing magic for your family is one thing, but performing for strangers sounds awful. Especially if you have to fake doing a bad job so you won't get in the show.

I kind of liked pulling off those two tricks!

I didn't like scaring Alfie, though. She's still acting shy around me.

"Hi, EllRay," Emma and Annie Pat say together

as they start up the slope. Emma has curly, tangled-looking hair, and like I've said before, Annie Pat wears her red hair in pigtails that look like orange highway cones.

"Is the grass wet?" Annie Pat asks. She catches cold a lot, I have noticed.

"Nah. It's mostly dry," I say.

"I have news," Emma tells Annie Pat and me as the other kids in our class start to arrive for our meeting. "Ms. Sanchez's wedding shower present from all the parents *is* going to be the fancy vacuum cleaner that was on their wish list. Some-body's mom got a good deal on one, so they finally all agreed."

"That's *tragic*," Annie Pat says, her dark blue eyes serious and sad. "They could have bought Ms. Sanchez the best aquarium in the world for that much money. Or even a saltwater aquarium."

Annie Pat wants to be a fish scientist when she grows up.

"But maybe vacuuming is something married people do together," Fiona says, a mushy look on her face. "Like dancing."

I can't picture it, but what do I know?

"Well, the deciding is over," Emma says, shaking her head. "Mom told me. All that's left is for us kids to make a card to go with it."

"Fiona can do that," Annie Pat says. "She's the best artist."

"No," I surprise myself by saying. "Everyone should write something for Ms. Sanchez. But maybe Fiona can draw the cover."

"You mean we should make a whole book?" Cynthia says. She has arrived quietly, for once, and has been listening in. "That sounds too hard."

"Maybe just one page from each of us?" I say, making it a question. "Something about getting married?"

Because I want to be part of this, even though I can't explain why. It just makes me sad to think of Ms. Sanchez getting married—and not being Ms. Sanchez anymore. The least I can do is help make her a wedding shower book.

"Good idea, EllRay," Emma says, smiling.

"We're here," Jared and Stanley shout, racing up the hill.

"Oh, good," Cynthia says, being sarcastic, which is her big thing. "That means we can start."

And her friend Heather snickers her approval of this put-down.

Fiona is inching up the sloping lawn as if each blade of grass is a hazard and her weak ankles might give way any second. She showed up! So her juggling raw eggs is out. Too bad.

"Who's gonna do what for the tryouts today?" I ask, getting straight to the point. "Everybody has to say one thing, whether you think it's any good or not. And then we can pick five acts."

"*DOINK, DOINK*," Stanley murmurs, fiddling with the imaginary crown on his floppy-haired head.

He's the one pretending to be bossy to me this time, in case you didn't get it.

"Quit doinking," Emma says.

"Me and Emma are taking ballet together," Annie Pat says. "We just started, but we can already do *pliés* and *tendus*. And *sautés*, because we're really good jumpers."

"We brought pretty music to play while we dance," Emma chimes in. "But our act only lasts one minute."

Cynthia does this huge pretend yawn, patting at her open mouth in a fake-ladylike way.

"Oh, yeah? Then what's your great talent?" Annie Pat challenges her.

"I'll sing 'The Star-Spangled Banner,' like superstars do before football and baseball games," Cynthia tells us. "And Heather will stand behind me holding an American flag, because that's not against her religion. We checked. And even if some people don't *love* it, they won't boo, because—it's 'The Star-Spangled Banner.'"

"I didn't know you could sing that well," Kry says, sounding interested.

"Me and Stanley are gonna dance, too," Jared informs everyone. "Hip-hop. That's our talent. We brought music."

Jared and Stanley dancing? They're so big and clumsy that it would be like watching Frankenstein's Monster and the Mummy trying to "bust a move," as my dad still says. I would actually pay money to see that! If I had any money left, that is.

"Okay, good," I say, writing it down. "Who's next?"

"I can recite a poem for everyone," Fiona says, peeping out the surprising words. "I write them myself. Mama likes me to say my poems when we have company. Only sometimes I cry, if it's a sad poem like the one I brought today," she confesses.

Fiona crying—while reading a poem—would be awesome. That would *definitely* not get in the talent show. I put a star next to her name. "Who's next?" I ask.

"I'm learning to juggle," Kry tells us. "But not eggs! And I'm not very good yet. I'm only up to two cotton balls at a time. You start with them because they're so light."

"Perfect," I say, drawing another star. Juggling one cotton ball would be even *better* for failing the tryouts, and juggling no balls would be the best. Kry could just stand there pretending to juggle! But you can't have everything.

"Okay," I say. "Who's left?"

"Kevin and Corey," Emma says.

"I won't be here Friday afternoon," Corey reports. "I have practice."

He works out almost every day at this swim center near San Diego. He does his homework in the car.

"You poor thing," Emma says, her eyes wide with pity.

"I think the buzzer's about to sound," Annie Pat

says, lifting her head as if she's got some sonar device inside it, like a dolphin does. She hates that buzzer.

"Kevin?" I ask.

"Stand-up," he says.

We all stare at him.

"You know," he tells us. "*Comedy*. I'll tell jokes. My dad helped me write some."

"Okay, good," I say, trying to hide my expression as I write it down. Because I like Kevin fine, don't get me wrong. In fact, he's still my half-best friend. But he cannot tell a joke. He always forgets part of it, sometimes even the ending. Or else he starts laughing in the middle of the joke and can't finish it.

"I'm good enough to flunk the tryouts, anyway," Kevin says, as if he's just read my mind. "What about you, EllRay?" he asks, like he wants to get back at me for doubting his comedy skills. "What's your talent, if you think you're so great?"

"I *don't* think I'm so great," I protest. "But I could do some magic, I guess."

"You don't know any magic," Jared scoffs.

"I know a little," I say. "Two illusions, so far.

Enough to look like I'm really trying, anyway."

"So, what five acts do we have?" Annie Pat asks, still braced for the buzzer.

"I think Fiona's poem, definitely," I say. "The sadder the better. And Kry's juggling act. And then maybe the hip-hop dance act?"

"Or ballet, only Emma and Annie Pat are probably too good not to get into the show," Kry says, sticking up for them.

"We'll skip it," Emma says, after sharing a quick look with Annie Pat.

"So that makes three so far," I say.

"**DOINK**," Stanley whispers again, telling everyone how bossy I'm being.

"Quit it," Emma tells him.

"You can't leave out 'The Star-Spangled Banner,' or it would be unpatriotic," Cynthia informs us, like she's really hoping to make it into that talent show.

"Okay. 'The Star-Spangled Banner,' complete with the American flag," I say.

"And EllRay's magic act," Jared says. "Because this I gotta see."

"Me too," Stanley says.

"Me three," Cynthia chimes in.

"Maybe EllRay can saw a girl in half," Corey says, staring her down. "We can vote on which girl."

"You better not," Cynthia says, narrowing her eyes.

"Believe me, I'm not that good," I tell her—and everyone.

But at least I've now got our class's five lame acts for the talent show tryouts. And they sound just lousy enough to fail—*if* I goof up my two illusions, that is.

"I want to tell my jokes," Kevin says, giving me a look.

Uh-oh! And we were partway back to being friends again.

"Okay," I say quickly. "We can probably have six acts. They sound short."

BZZZ–Z–Z!

The morning buzzer sounds, and poor Annie Pat just about jumps out of her skin. She startles easily, Emma says.

And we all head for class.

✻ 9 ✻

THE TRYOUTS

"I'm impressed, EllRay," Ms. Sanchez says after taking attendance. She is holding the list I just handed her. "You kids said you could get this sorted out by yourselves, and you did—with an act to spare, I see," she tells us. And she reads the following list aloud.

1. Jared and Stanley dance very cool hip hop!

2. Fiona recites this really sad poem she wrote!

3. Kevin tells jokes that are so funny he could be on cable TV!

4. Kry juggles awesome cotton balls!

5. Cynthia sings the very patriotic 'Star-Spangled Banner' while Heather holds the American flag!

6. EllRay does two magic illusions!

"It sounds amazing," Ms. Sanchez says. "And, mercy, so many exclamation points! I had no idea this class was such a hotbed of talent. And you all have your supplies with you? Music, magic tricks, and so on?"

Eight of us nod, suddenly solemn.

This is real.

I'll need a little table, but everything else is in my lunch bag.

"Good. Our class's tryout time is at eleven a.m., before lunch," Ms. Sanchez tells us. "They're giving us forty-five minutes, and the entire class is invited to attend. You'll all go straight to lunch from there, so bring your cafeteria money or your lunch boxes with you. But no eating in the auditorium," she reminds us.

What about throwing up in the auditorium, Ms. Sanchez? I ask silently.

Because—*I'm nervous.* I thought we'd just get turned down in private, with only a few witnesses, and that would be it. No talent show. Now, though, our whole class will be watching the tryouts. *And* Ms. Sanchez. But I'm supposed to fail?

How embarrassing.

Is it too late to back out now?

A couple of the other tryout kids are looking as if they'd also like to change their minds, but it's too late.

"Shhh," Ms. Sanchez says at five minutes before eleven a.m. as she hustles us down the hall toward the auditorium. "Classes are in session, people."

"It's cool walking in the hall when no one else is here," Emma whispers, and Annie Pat and Kry nod.

I agree, but my heart is pounding too hard for me to react to what she just said.

And—we enter the almost-empty auditorium.

The judges are sitting in the front row, on one side of the main aisle. First, there's our bearded principal, Mr. James, whose name I usually forget—possibly due to the shock of having been called into his office *twice* this year.

Next to him, there's the lady singing teacher who comes around to Oak Glen Primary School, but not as often as she used to, because of money.

She has long gray hair and wears dangly earrings and swishy skirts.

Next to her are two strange grown-ups who are probably talented people who live in Oak Glen. The lady has big, fancy yellow hair, like one of Alfie's dolls, but kind of an old-lady face. The man is almost an antique. He looks as if he's wearing some bigger guy's suit. His little white-haired head pokes out of his white, button-down shirt like a turtle's head coming out of its shell.

I hope we can trust them to reject us from the talent show!

Ms. Sanchez seats us on the left side of the aisle and hands my list to the principal, who looks it over, smiles, and nods. Ms. Sanchez hurries around the row and takes her seat next to the turtle-man in the too-big suit.

The principal stands up. "Welcome, third-graders," he announces. "These are our judges," he says, waving at the people sitting in his row. "Let's give them a rousing Oak Glen thank-you with a big round of applause."

So we clap our hands as loud—and as long—as we can.

✳ **10** ✳

TO MAKE A LONG STORY SHORT

"And now," the principal says, glancing at a piece of paper, "we'll start with Jared Matthews and Stanley Washington, who are going to dance to '*Big Ole*—'" he pauses a second—"'*Bottom*.'"

A couple of girls gasp, recognizing the song, and some of the boys start to **CRACK UP**, remembering its real title.

"You'll change your music selection, please, if you happen to get in," the principal says over the uproar as Jared and Stanley stomp up the stairs at the side of the stage.

"Okay. And we'll wear different pants, too," Jared says. "Bigger, lower ones."

"We'll see," the principal says, raising his hairy eyebrows.

Stanley hands a CD to a lady standing near a

table at the edge of the stage. "Not too loud, Miss Myrna," the principal calls out to her, and she nods.

BOOM. BOOM. BOOM. The music starts up, and then the dancing starts—with kick backs, heel hops, and a lot of swag and foot action. Who knew Jared and Stanley had it in them? They're not like Frankenstein's Monster or the Mummy at all! They must have been taking lessons or something. Is that cheating?

Stanley's got the "Stanky Legg" down cold. He's keeping his knees bent really low, and it looks like he's skating, his legs seem so rubbery and smooth. His feet never leave the floor. He's keeping those moves clean. He looks sharp. Stanley! Of all people!

And Jared's "Dougie" is good, too. He's down low, and his feet are shifting just right. His arms are pumping and pushing perfectly, swinging loose as they chop through the air. They move so far behind him they seem to be about to wrap around his body. But he's not grabbing himself, which would mean getting rejected for sure.

Stanley ends by taking hold of one foot and

hopping over it with his whole body—*almost.* He stumbles, but just a little.

At the same time, Jared ends with a little "Wheelchair" action, dropping, dropping his knees as he circles his arms. Then he falls to the stage and whirls around on one beefy shoulder for their combined big finish.

And "*Yay-y-y!*" we all cheer, clapping like crazy—partly because they were so good, and partly because we're surprised. Stanley pulls Jared up off the floor, and they pretend bow and then shamble toward the stairs.

"Dude! Dude!" Kevin high-fives each of them as they take their seats again.

"All right. Settle down," the principal says, smiling. And we go on to our class's next five acts.

To make a long story short, Fiona's poem didn't work out very well—though it started okay. "This is a poem I wrote called 'The Death of Fuzzers,' by Fiona McNulty," she began. "Fuzzers was my hamster who passed away," she explained, her eyes already filling with tears.

> *"Oh, darling Fuzzers, why did you have to go and die?*
> *Are you now a furry angel way up in the sky?"*

And that was about as far as she got before she started to sob.

I'll admit that was entertaining for us kids, the boys, anyway, but I don't think the judges liked it much. Miss Myrna had to go searching for some tissues, though.

Fiona and her weak ankles barely made it

down the stairs. Cynthia and Heather rushed over to help her to her seat, though, and Fiona looked happy about that. They patted her shoulders and whispered her back to normal.

Kevin's jokes didn't work out, either. He kept saying stuff like, "No, wait! I forgot to tell you that the man was a *clown*, see." That kind of thing. And he *did* start laughing during his last joke, which came at the end of the longest three minutes in our earth's history. I felt so bad for him.

But we all clapped anyway, and Kevin looked like he thought it went pretty well. He was still laughing at his last joke when he sat down.

Kry's juggling act—complete with these two cotton balls the size of marshmallows—turned into a comedy act, really, because she couldn't keep even the two cotton puffs in the air. But she talked the whole time she was trying to juggle, and she was so funny that the judges were laughing their heads off, even the little old guy with the white hair, who almost fell out of his seat. Ms. Sanchez had to grab him! He looked like he hadn't laughed that hard in fifty years.

Kry finished with the biggest curtsy you ever

saw, and all us kids clapped hard as she came bouncing down the stairs.

The "Star-Spangled Banner" act was okay, except you could barely hear Cynthia's puny singing voice over the blare of the CD Miss Myrna put on. And when Miss Myrna turned down the music, it got worse, because then you *could* hear Cynthia's voice. Also, she kept repeating the same lines, which even I knew was wrong.

"And the rocket's red glare!
And the rocket's red glare,
And the ro-o-ocket's red glare,
And the rocket's red glare . . ."

The flag at the corner of the stage was too big and heavy for Heather to hold, so she stood behind Cynthia the whole time Cynthia sang, *pretending* to wave a flag, a serious and patriotic expression on her face. I was afraid she might cry, too, she was so into it.

"I'll learn the real words for the show," Cynthia announced to the judges after our polite spatter of applause was over.

But by that point, I was so nervous I could barely think straight.

Because *I was up next.*

I got an old red pencil case—for my magic supplies—out of my lunch bag with cold, numb fingers, and I prepared to climb those stairs. Part of me had changed plans and wanted to get into the talent show after all, and part of me wanted to flub my tricks and get rejected, as planned.

But *all* of me wanted to get it over with.

The principal stood again as we clapped for Cynthia and Heather, who looked pink and happy—as if they thought they'd done a pretty good job.

"And finally, we have the magic that is EllRay Jakes," the principal said, giving me a too-big introduction, considering what was in my little red pencil case. "So put your hands together for EllRay the Magnificent!"

Oh, great, I thought. Now I'm *magnificent*? Like I'm gonna be able to live that one down!

Man, I was hoping I wouldn't drop those quarters or accidentally cut the string.

✵ 11 ✵

THAT SPECIAL BOOK

It is Tuesday morning, and the lady in our school office just posted the list for Friday afternoon's talent show on the bulletin board next to her office door.

I GOT IN THE SHOW.

Oh. No.

Jared and Stanley got in, too. They are whooping and high-fiving each other like crazy in the hall, shouting "Dude" and "Dog!" while Kevin tells everyone who walks by the good news.

I feel numb from the top of my hair down to the end of my toenails.

See, I was so sure I *didn't* get in. After I did my first trick, the lady judge with the blonde hair asked me if I could make my coin trick bigger, so people at the back of the audience could see it better. That's when I lost the tiny piece of hope about getting in I had secretly been holding onto, because—what did that lady think? That since I had created two quarters out of a dime in front of her very eyes, why not make two Frisbees out of a little round plate so kids in the back row could see the illusion better?

Yeah, lady! I can do my coin trick bigger—*when my hands grow giant-sized.*

That's what I should have said.

But I'm too polite, thanks to my parents.

Instead, I stared at my feet and shook my head *no.*

"Well, it was a wonderful trick anyway," she said, trying to cheer me up.

Luckily, nothing went wrong with the "Cut String Made Whole" illusion. And the blonde lady didn't ask me if I could do it with a rope and a hose instead, so everyone could see better.

I guess I could, *if my hands were still huge, lady.*

I was so *sure* I hadn't gotten in!

"Congratulations, EllRay," Emma says as Annie Pat smiles.

"Yeah," Corey says. "I was really worried, but

I knew you'd do it, dude. Your tricks were awesome. As much as I could tell from the third row, anyway. Sorry I'm gonna miss the show," he adds, looking sad.

"Thanks," I croak.

"I couldn't see your act very well," Heather complains. "Especially your first trick. And I was in the *second* row."

"I couldn't see either one," Kevin says. "But magic is cool, and so is EllRay. So it's good he got in."

Kevin is probably feeling generous because Jared and Stanley are so happy. I wish he was still my whole-best friend, instead of just being half-best. "Thanks," I tell him, trying to smile.

Only four more days until the talent show, when almost no one will be able to see my lame illusions. But even though part of me is horrified I got in, another part is feeling tingly and warm, like something truly magical has happened.

I wish there was such a thing as real magic!

If I were a wizard, for example, I could truly astound even the biggest and hairiest sixth-grader on Friday—instead of doing two beginner's tricks they either already know or won't be able to see.

They'll probably all be whispering and texting during my act, even though that's not allowed.

Who cares? Not me.

And I kind of can't wait to tell my dad I got in the show.

Maybe he'll be proud of me!

"We'd better decide about that special book for Ms. Sanchez. You know, the one EllRay thought up," Emma says during afternoon recess. Most of us are standing around the tetherball corner of the playground, though Jared and Stanley are trying to teach some guys a couple of hip-hop moves near the fence. "The wedding shower is this Friday, after the talent show," Emma reminds us. "Fiona already said she'd do the cover."

"I think I'll draw Ms. Sanchez in her bride costume," Fiona says, sounding shyer than she should for someone who is so good at art. "And I might glue real lace around the edges of the book."

"Ooo. Real lace," Annie Pat says, her voice soft.

"I think our pages should all be the same size,

or else our book will look like babies did it," I say, hitting the tetherball hard enough for it to twirl around the pole three times. One-person tetherball!

"Yeah," Emma agrees. "Like, notebook-paper size. Okay?"

"Look who's trying to boss everyone around," Cynthia tells Heather, but you can tell that she's not all that into picking a fight with Emma, who is usually her favorite target. Not today. I think she really wanted to get in that talent show.

Wanna trade places with *me*, Cynthia?

"Emma's not bossing anyone," Kry says. "What do you think Ms. Sanchez's book should be about, Cynthia?" she asks, like she actually wants to know. Maybe she *does* want to know. Kry's that nice. Or maybe she's trying to make Cynthia feel better about the talent show.

"I don't know," Cynthia says, shrugging as if she's too busy to think about it much. "We could write down recipes, only none of us can cook."

"Except for s'mores on camping trips," Kry says, taking her turn whacking the tetherball.

Emma looks thoughtful. "What about if we each

say something we like about Ms. Sanchez?" she suggests.

"Naw," Corey says. "Too kiss-uppy."

"Huh," Annie Pat says. "There's a difference between kissing up and being *nice*, Corey. And if you can't be nice to someone at their wedding shower, when can you be nice?"

"That's right," Emma agrees.

"I think we should say something to Ms. Sanchez about getting married," I say.

Like "Don't do it," I add silently. I like her the way she is.

"What do we know about being married?" Annie Pat asks, blinking her dark blue eyes.

"Lots, really," I tell her—and everyone. "We all have moms and dads, don't we? Some kids have even more than two parents," I add, thinking of the stepmoms and stepdads that a few kids in my class have. Like Emma, whose father lives in some foreign country with a new wife. She told me once.

"Yeah," everyone standing there mumbles.

"And aren't we spying on them all the time, basically?" I ask.

"Not *snooping* spying," Kry says, frowning.

"No," I agree. "Nothing weird. But we see what's going on with them, and we have ideas about what they do, and the way they are. I'm just saying we should maybe pass those ideas along. You know, to help Ms. Sanchez when she—"

"But she has her own mom and dad to tell her stuff about getting married," Cynthia interrupts, which is something she often does.

"That's only two people," I point out. "Old people. But if all of us told Ms. Sanchez just one important thing about being a married lady, she'd have a *ton* of good advice."

"We could do both," Kry says, coming up with the perfect answer, as usual. "We could each say something we like about her, number one, and number two, give her advice about getting married, the way EllRay said."

"That sounds *hard*," Heather says, copying Cynthia's complaint from the other day.

"It's just two sentences on a piece of notebook paper, Heather," I say. "That's like *nothing*. And you have four days to do it."

"Three days at the most," Fiona corrects me.

"Because I have to put the book together all nice after I get the pages."

Oh, yeah. I guess Fiona's in charge of that part because she's doing the cover.

"Okay, three days," I say. "That means we have to turn in our pages by Thursday, right? So they'll be ready in time for the party on Friday? But everyone in class has to do a page, and we have to keep it a secret from Ms. Sanchez—*and* our parents, or they'll take over the whole thing."

Emma and Annie Pat pinch their lips shut, making Xs across them with their pointer fingers like they've been practicing this secrecy sign for ages.

"She'll like our book much better than any *vacuum cleaner*," Corey says.

"It's not a contest between presents," Cynthia reminds him.

"Yeah, but she will," Corey insists.

And I think he's right.

Who likes to vacuum?

Even when they can do it together, like dancing.

✳ **12** ✳

MAKING THINGS OKAY WITH ALFIE

"Knock, knock," I say, standing in the doorway of Alfie's room that night.

"Who's there?" Alfie asks, sounding wary as she looks up from where she is sitting on her rug. She is combing a pink plastic horse's tail, a tail that is so long it trails behind it on the ground like a fancy bride cape, or whatever that thing is called. I wonder if Ms. Sanchez will wear one of those at her wedding to that guy?

I know his name, but I'm not gonna say it.

Alfie looks like she's still scared of **MAGIC** me. She didn't talk much during dinner.

It was kind of relaxing, I have to say.

"What do you mean, 'Who's there?'" I ask. "It's me, EllRay. Your *brother*. I'm standing right here. You're looking at me," I say, trying to sound as normal and unmagical as possible.

Making things okay with Alfie has to happen fast, Mom told me after dinner. She says the whole family is a nervous wreck because of Alfie getting freaked out by magic.

1. For the past two nights, she has gone to bed only if all the lights in her room stay on. All night long.

2. She made Mom lock up the bunny hand puppet I gave her—the one that was in my magic set—in the safe in my dad's office. And that bunny never did a *thing* to deserve being locked up! I think he needs a bunny lawyer.

3. Nobody is supposed to say the word "magic" around Alfie, either.

4. Even her braids have started to droop.

"Oh," Alfie says, sounding disappointed. "I thought you were doing a knock-knock joke. What do you want? Don't come in."

"Why not?" I ask.

"Because this is pwivate pwoperty," Alfie says, fluffing up her horse's tail.

That's Alfie-speak for "private property."

"But I want to show you something," I tell her. "Something secret and cool."

"What?" she asks.

"How I do my two tricks," I say, taking one step inside her pink and purple room. My red pencil case is tucked into the back of my pants, which is where TV detectives sometimes hide their guns.

That sounds risky to me.

Calling my magic "tricks" instead of "illusions" will work better with Alfie, I think. They sound less spooky that way.

"I don't wanna see any more magic," Alfie mumbles, staring down as she fiddles with the circle of tiny flowers around her horse's head. "So go away."

"I'll let you keep the coins after I show you the first trick," I say, bribing her. And this might work, because money is Alfie's new hobby, almost. She has been saving up for a Golden Sparkle Corral for her plastic horses for *ages*. She'll probably be twenty years old before she has enough money for it, and who would want a Golden Sparkle Corral then?

I take another step toward her.

"Don't stand on my wug, EllWay, or I'll call the police," Alfie warns me. "And who wants magic money that a person can't even spend?"

"It's regular money," I say. "You can spend it just

fine. I'll even give you an extra quarter if you let me show you how I do the trick. See, I can't really turn a dime into two quarters. I just end the trick by hiding the dime *behind* one of the quarters."

"Like how?" she asks, looking suspicious.

"Like this," I say. And I kneel at the edge of her rug, whisk out my pencil case, arrange the three coins in my hand, and show her every step of the first trick, including dropping the quarters a few times by mistake.

"*Abracadabra*," I say, and I hand her the coins.

"So you were just fooling me?" Alfie asks, scowling.

"Yeah," I say. "But *fun*-fooling you. That's what tricks are. I wasn't being mean."

"What about that other quarter you said I could have?" she asks, looking less worried than when I first walked into her room, I'm glad to see.

"I don't have it on me, but I won't forget to give it to you. I promise," I say.

"Okay. But cutting the *stwing* was real, right?" she asks. "And then putting it back together again?"

"No. That was a trick, too. Want to see?"

"I guess," she says. And I move onto her fluffy

rug, get out my supplies, and show them to her—including the straw with the slit in it. And then I do the trick, making sure she sees how I pull the looped string down before I cut the straw.

"Huh," Alfie says, looking as thoughtful as a four-year-old can. "So you were faking the whole time?"

"That's what tricks are," I explain. "The fun part comes from being amazed, and maybe from trying to figure out how the person did the trick."

"I didn't know there *was* a fun part," Alfie says. "But is that why you were bwagging at dinner? Because you're gonna fool everyone at the talent show?"

"I wasn't *bragging*," I say. "I was telling Mom and Dad. It was just conversation."

"And telling me," Alfie says.

"And telling you. But do you want to know a secret?"

"Sure. What?" Alfie says, and her brown eyes sparkle. She loves secrets almost as much as she loves chocolate.

"I might try getting out of the whole thing to-morrow. It's making me nervous."

"How can you get out of it?"

"I'll talk to the principal," I say, making my mind up on the spot, right there on Alfie's rug. And the pastel plastic horses with long goofy tails that drag on the floor are my witnesses.

"But you're *scared* of your principal," Alfie says, her eyes wide. "He's all hairy, like a wee-wuff."

She means "werewolf," but that's really hard for her to say.

"It's just his beard that makes him look that way," I assure her. "And I'm scared of getting in trouble at *school*, I'm not scared of *him*," I add, trying to explain. "He's not that bad. He knows all our names, even. He must practice them at night. Probably with flash cards," I add, thinking about it. That's what I would do.

I have trouble remembering *his* name—even though there's only one of him.

Maybe I should just call him "Your Honor"? Like on TV?

Our principal always stands on the school's front steps in the morning to greet us. That will be my big chance to explain why my two small magic illusions won't work in our school auditorium.

"You're bwave," Alfie tells me, moving in for a snuggle.

"Not really," I say, letting her give me a sweaty little hug.

"You are," she says, sounding fierce, like she's sticking up for me.

"Well, I think you're brave, too," I say. "Like, how you usually sleep with the lights out and stuff. And you're only four. That's awesome."

"I *used to* do that," she says, as if it were a long time ago, not just last week.

"Maybe you could do it again someday," I say, shrugging like it's no big deal either way.

Well, it isn't. Not to me.

"Maybe I will," she agrees. "But not tonight." She gives me another **SQUEEZE**, though.

"Whenever," I tell her.

Mom's going to be so *relieved*.

"But you still owe me a quarter, EllWay," Alfie says. "You pwomised."

"Okay," I say, springing to my feet. "I'll go get it *right now*."

Anything to escape all this mush!

✳ **13** ✳

TELLING DAD

Telling Dad that I decided I want to drop out of Oak Glen's talent show is going to be hard. He and my mom are probably still celebrating because they're so amazed I got in!

They like to hang out in the family room after dinner, even though they don't watch much TV. In fact, they do different things. Usually Dad reads, because college geology professors have lots of stuff "to wade through," as he puts it. Mom likes to watch TV shows and movies on her tablet. But she wears ear buds so the noise won't bother my dad.

At least they're together in the same room, my mom says when I ask why they don't just do the stuff they like in different places.

I hate ear buds. They make my ear holes hot and sore. I want really cool headphones.

See, that's what I should say on my page of Ms. Sanchez's wedding shower book:

Watch out, because getting married means you will never get to do exactly what you want, the way you want, ever again!

Instead, I'll have to make up something nice. I don't want to make Ms. Sanchez sad on her wedding shower day.

I am *never* getting married. What if the lady I married didn't like *Die, Creature, Die*, my favorite video game? What then?

I won't give up my game just for you, whoever-you-are!

"Hi, honey," Mom says, spotting me standing in the doorway, watching them. "Did you manage to talk some sense into your sister?"

"Mm-hmm," I say, nodding. "She's better, I think. I showed her how the tricks work, so she doesn't think I have magical powers anymore."

I leave out the part about paying her off with the coins, because Mom and Dad would not approve of that. But I still think it was a good idea.

"Good," Dad says, smiling as he looks up from his book. "Maybe things will get back to what passes for normal around here."

"Alfie's going to sleep in the dark again," I tell them. "Only not tonight."

"Well, baby steps are better than no steps at all," my dad says, shrugging.

"But speaking of magic," I say before he can dive back into his book, "can I talk to you about something important, Dad? I mean, *may* I?"

Because my dad is gonna hear about it, if the principal lets me drop out of the show. He and Mom might even have been planning to come watch! So I'd better tell him now, and get it over with. He's the one who taught me the illusions.

"In my office?" Dad asks, tilting his head.

"Sure," I say.

At least Mom will be able to listen to her show for a while without those ear buds ruining the whole thing.

"What's up, son?" Dad asks after we sit down.

"It's about the talent show," I say, staring down at my bony knees. "I think I have to drop out. My tricks are too **SMALL** for a whole assembly to see. I'm going to tell the principal tomorrow morning. I just wanted to let you know."

"Hmm. Stage fright?" my dad asks, frowning.

"No," I say, shaking my head. "And those illusions were *good*. But like I said, they were meant for just a few people at a time, not a whole auditorium full."

"I was wondering about that," Dad admits. "I knew they'd get you through the tryouts, but . . ."

"But they won't work for the real show," I finish, since he has stopped talking. "I would look like a fool, and all the big kids would laugh at me—or boo me off the stage. My reputation would be ruined— and I have *three more years* at Oak Glen."

"You're exaggerating," Dad says, using the calm, reasonable voice that usually means I've already lost the argument.

"I'm not exaggerating," I tell him. "It would be like—like I was some weirdo meteorite from outer space that didn't fit in," I say, trying to explain in a way he can understand. "You know," I add. "When all the other kids were normal earth rocks. And I just barely fit in *now*."

"Wait. What? You feel like you don't fit in at Oak Glen?" my dad asks, a concerned look on his face. There is a new, sharp note in his voice.

He thinks I'm talking about being one of the few kids with brown skin at my school! He can get real touchy about stuff like that.

This is exactly the kind of thing he worries about. We're going way past magic tricks here. I have to get us back on track, and fast.

"I fit in okay," I assure him. "But I won't, if I'm forced to make a fool out of myself."

"So why did they ask you to be in the show?" Dad asks, frowning.

"That's what I can't figure out!" I say, the words almost falling out of my mouth. "Because like I said, nobody will be able to see what I'm doing! I guess it's because I was the only one in the show."

"The only one?" my dad asks, his voice tight again.

"The only *magician*," I tell him as calmly as I can.

GEEZ.

"But you like doing magic," he says, like he's trying to get something straight inside his brain.

"Yes," I say. "More than I thought I would. And like I said, those are good tricks to do," I add, since, he was the one who found them and taught me how to do them. "But not in front of the whole school at once."

"So you wouldn't mind being in the show if you had better—bigger—tricks," he says, still figuring it out.

"But I don't," I say. "And the show is this Friday afternoon."

"Want me to talk to the principal for you?" Dad asks. "Explain things?"

"No, thanks," I say. "I'd better do it myself. Tomorrow morning. He'll understand."

Maybe.

But the last thing I need is my dad making a big deal out of this.

"Are you disappointed?" I ask him, even though

the question makes me feel kind of shy. "You know, that I won't be in the show?"

"Not at all, son," Dad says, giving me a smile. "Because you would be stepping aside for a logical reason, not because you were scared."

He still sounds proud of me!

"I'd be a *little* scared, even if everything went right," I admit.

"That's only natural," my dad says, smiling again. "In fact, stage fright is probably the mark of a great performer."

I think about it for a second. "I wouldn't say those tricks were *great*, exactly," I finally tell him, trying to be honest. "Or that I'm such an amazing magician. Not yet, anyway."

Dad nods his agreement. "These things take time, EllRay," he says. "That, and the right equipment, and a whole lot of practice."

"So, you'll tell Mom what I decided?" I ask, looking at my knees again.

I hate the thought of disappointing my mom— more than anything, just about.

"I'll take care of it," Dad says. "Why don't you go

on upstairs and jump in the shower? I have a few things to take care of in here, and then I'll come tuck you and Alfie in."

"But don't say anything to Alfie about leaving the lights on," I remind him. "Because I think she needs at least one more night before she backs down."

"Got it," my dad says with one quick nod. "See, I do listen to you, son. Now, scoot."

And I scoot.

✳ **14** ✳

MAN-TO-MAN

Grown-ups call Wednesday "Hump Day" because it's in the middle of the Monday to Friday work week. You have to get over it—the invisible "hump"—to be able to coast down the other side of the hill toward Friday and, best of all, the weekend.

I think it's the same for kids, because Wednesday mornings are always a pain.

1. It's hard to get up on time.

2. It's hard to pry your little sister out of the bathroom so you can at least brush your teeth.

3. It's hard to find a shirt you want to wear that's clean, or nearly clean.

4. It's hard to get all your school stuff together so you don't forget anything and get in trouble in front of the whole class.

But today, Wednesday, I wanted to get to school early enough to talk to the principal, so I pulled it together. And here I am, one of many kids swarming up Oak Glen Primary School's wide front steps.

And there *he* is, planted right in the center of the middle step where he "sees all," as he sometimes tells us at assemblies. "Mr. Jakes!" he calls out through his beard.

But today, instead of ducking my head, waving hello, and hurrying past him, as usual, I stop.

"Penny! David. Hey, Kelli, what's up? Bryce," the principal is calling out. "What's happening, Mai? What's shakin', bacon?"

I clear my throat a couple of times, the way my half-friend Kevin sometimes does to get attention. But the principal can't hear me **AHEM-ING** over the roar that surrounds us. "Excuse me," I say, but my voice is still too quiet for him to hear.

"Looking good, Leonard," he yells. "Morning, Miss Daisy Liu!"

"Excuse me, Your Honor," I shout in a way-too-loud voice. A couple of older kids turn, point, and laugh.

So does the principal. "'*Your Honor*,'" he says

like he's quoting me. "That's a good one, EllRay! You're priceless, d'you know that? How can I help you, son?"

"I can't be in the talent show on Friday," I tell him louder than I'd like to.

"And why is that?" he asks, focusing his famous laser-beam look at me. "Cold feet?"

"Huh?"

"Stage fright," he explains, telling me what the expression means.

Oh. That's what Dad thought, too. And he was right, even if I didn't admit it.

"No," I tell the principal, staring at his beard to make talking to him easier. "It's because my two illusions are meant for small groups, like one or two people, not a big assembly. No one will be able to see them. So I have to—to step aside," I say, using my dad's words. "Sorry," I add, trying to look like I mean it.

"And yet you tried out for the show with those two tricks," the principal points out, petting his beard.

"I had to think up something fast," I explain. "I mean, the whole talent show idea *was* kind of last-minute."

Wait. Does that sound like I'm criticizing him?

"I like to come up with something fun for my students toward the end of the year, when things start to sag a little," the principal tells me, like he's talking man to man. "Only there's no money left in the PTA Special Events Fund. So a talent show seemed like a good option."

"You mean because it's *free*," I say. "That's fine, except my illusions won't work. Like I said before, they're too small. So I'll have to step aside," I tell him again.

I like saying "step aside." It sounds better than "quit."

"No one's going to be stepping *anywhere* at this point, except onto the auditorium stage this Friday afternoon," the principal says, a that's-that look settling on his hairy face. "And you're our show's only magic act," he adds. "Don't worry, EllRay. You'll do fine. Just relax."

Whenever someone tells you to "just relax," exactly the opposite happens.

So far, Hump Day isn't going so great.

"I *won't* do fine," I say, not backing down. "I'll do *awful*. And I can't relax! I'll be a flop. Everyone will

laugh at me, or boo me off the stage. And I'll never live it down, ever—for three more years. Even *my dad* understands," I add, bringing out my best ammunition. Because I think the only thing that really counts with teachers and principals is kids' parents.

And that's messed up.

"Your dad," the principal says, echoing my words.

"Dr. Warren Jakes," I remind him.

They've talked before. The principal looks like he's getting a headache.

He sighs. "Well, EllRay, I understand what you're saying, and I'm sorry," he says. "I'd like to let you off the hook, believe me. But the program is already being printed up, and your name's on it."

That's no reason at all! Programs are just pieces of paper, and I'm a *person*. "You could make an announcement saying sorry, but there's no time for my magic act," I say, almost begging, as a couple of sixth-graders shove past me.

DO. NOT. CRY, I tell myself, making it an order.

"Tell you what," the principal says. "When I introduce your act, I will explain about the tricks being meant for smaller venues. And then you can go ahead and do them."

Venues? Now, I don't know *what* he's saying—except that he's not gonna let me out of this stupid talent show.

"And rest easy," the principal assures me. "No one is going to boo. Not at *my* school."

His students. *His* school. What is up with this guy?

"I really don't wanna do it," I say, my voice barely there. "Please don't make me."

"What was that?" the principal says, cupping a big hand behind one of his ears as he leans over to get down to my shrimpy level. "I didn't hear that last part."

"Nothing," I mumble. "It was nothing."

I'm nothing. He's not even *trying* to understand. And he thinks he's such a great principal, saying hi to everyone!

"Then you'd better run along to class," he tells me. "And don't worry about Friday, EllRay. You'll do *great*."

✳ 15 ✳

SOME VERY GOOD ADVICE

"Okay," Fiona says, taking charge for once, even though she is usually the shyest kid in our class. It is Thursday lunch, which is the deadline to hand in our pages for Ms. Sanchez's wedding shower book. We are all huddled around the girls' picnic table. "Who goes first?" she asks.

"Here's mine," Kry says, putting a piece of paper on Fiona's sweater, which she has spread on the table to keep our pages clean.

"What's your wedding advice?" Cynthia asks. Kry is the only girl Cynthia looks up to. I guess that's why she asked.

"It says, *'Play outside with your husband every day,'*" Kry reports. "But what I wrote about why I like Ms. Sanchez is private."

Good, I think—because I feel the same way.

"I'll go next," Heather says, eager to get it over

with. "My advice is, *'Don't ever cut your hair short. My mom says that men love long hair.'*"

Huh. I never knew ladies had official ideas about stuff like that.

"Next?" Fiona asks.

Kevin clears his throat. "Here's my advice," he says. "*'Save up. Don't spend all your money.'* My dad helped me with that one," he adds, making a face.

Ms. Sanchez and that guy she's marrying—okay, *Mr. Timberlake*, but the one who runs a sporting goods store, not the famous one—both have jobs, so they must already be pretty rich. But whatever.

"Good," Fiona says, straightening the pile of papers as if she's the teacher. "Stanley?"

"I think Ms. Sanchez saw him writing it this morning," Cynthia says, tattling.

"She did not," Stanley says, glaring at Cynthia through his smudged glasses. "Anyway, mind your own business. My advice is, *'Make chocolate chip cookies for Mr. Timberlake every week.'*"

I think that's some very good advice. *Excellent* advice. And oatmeal cookies are good, too—if you leave out the raisins.

"Corey?" Fiona asks.

"Okay," Corey says, blushing underneath his freckles. "My advice says, *'Call your husband "honey" and "sweetie" and "darling" a lot, in case you forget his name.'*"

"Ooo, 'darling,'" Stanley jeers. "*Smoochy, smoochy,*" he adds, kissing his hand.

"You and your hand," I say, teasing him. Corey's my best friend, so Stanley should lay off. "What's up with that? Are you in love with your hand, Stanley? Kissy, kissy, kissy?"

A couple of girls giggle.

"Shut up, EllRay," Stanley mumbles, even though we aren't allowed to say that.

"Yeah. Shut up," Jared says. "Here's my advice for Ms. Sanchez. *'Don't fight in front of your kids.'*"

I feel kind of bad about that one, because Jared's parents *do* fight in front of their kids. And their kids' friends. I heard them do it once. I wanted to go home—and I hugged my own mom and dad when I got there.

"That's a good one," I tell Jared.

"What's yours?" Jared challenges me, in case

I'm making fun of him—which I'm not.

I am instantly so embarrassed that my ears buzz. But of course this won't be anywhere near as bad as the talent show tomorrow, I remind myself. "My advice says, *'Learn how to play your husband's favorite video games. And do whatever you want at night,'*" I add, thinking of my parents.

"Also good ones," Corey congratulates me.

"No, they aren't," Heather scoffs. "They're *opposites*! Because how is Ms. Sanchez going to play her husband's video games *and* do whatever she wants at night? He should do what *she* wants, for a change."

"She could do both," Corey says, defending me. "Maybe playing video games is what Ms. Sanchez really likes to do."

I kinda don't think so. But I still think she could follow both pieces of advice.

"Cynthia?" Fiona says, probably to change the subject—even though she's usually so scared of her that she almost turns invisible when Cynthia and Heather are around. I guess being chosen to do the fancy cover for our class's book has made her braver, somehow.

"Okay," Cynthia says, looking important. "Here's *my* advice. *'Instead of saying, "For richer or poorer, for better or worse," which my mom says is in the wedding vows, you should say, "For richer and richer, for better and better." Because why go asking for trouble?'*"

"Good advice," her assistant Heather says, nodding her head.

Which proves that she would congratulate Cynthia on *anything*.

"But it's *long* advice," Emma says, frowning. "And I don't think you can go changing stuff that's in the Bible," she adds.

"It's not *in* the Bible," Cynthia tells her, her nose in the air. "Heather checked. Someone just made it up. What's your wedding advice for Ms. Sanchez, if you're so smart?"

"Mine is, *'Get lots of pets so you can practice for having babies,'*" Emma tells us. "Because I think they should have more than one. Baby, I mean."

Emma is an only child, she told me once. I guess that's why she thinks that.

I should lend her Alfie for a while.

Annie Pat laughs. "That's funny," she says. "Because my advice is, *'Go to the beach whenever you can. And only have one baby.'*"

And Annie Pat's mom has a baby at home!

Annie Pat and Emma are best friends, but they gave **OPPOSITE** advice about having babies. That's strange.

"And here's my advice," Fiona says. "*'Always wear darling shoes.'*"

"Good one," Emma says, smiling.

The girls in our class are all big fans of Ms. Sanchez's clothes—especially her shoes, which are mostly high heels.

"Everyone who hasn't turned their paper in yet has to get it to me by the end of the day," Fiona announces to the rest of the kids. "Or they won't be in the book. But don't let Ms. Sanchez catch you writing stuff down," she warns. "Or you'll wreck the secret."

"What about the cover?" Cynthia asks. "Let's see it."

"You can't, because it isn't done yet," Fiona says.

"The glue for the lace and pearls hasn't dried. But I'm finishing it tonight."

"Ooh. Lace and *pearls*," Annie Pat says, her eyes wide.

"You *better* finish," Cynthia says, just to keep in practice for being mean, I guess.

"Yeah," Heather says. "I second that. Maybe we should vote on it."

"Nah," Cynthia says, and Heather blushes.

Jared looks worried.

"What's the matter?" I ask him.

"I dunno," he says, shaking his big head. "I think some of our advice is kind of weird."

"Well, but so are we," Emma says, laughing.

"You, maybe," Cynthia says.

"It's okay," I tell Jared. "Ms. Sanchez is pretty much used to us. I think she'll *expect* weird."

"And she'll love the book," Kry—the optimist—assures him.

"Yeah," Jared grumbles. "She'll like it the way some parents say they like their kids' scribble-scrabbles, when they put them up on the fridge with magnets. But everyone will laugh at us."

"They might laugh," I say, thinking more about the talent show than the wedding shower book. "But it's too late now to do anything else. So just forget about it, dude."

"Don't tell me what to do," Jared says, making himself look big, which isn't hard.

"Maybe I wasn't talking to you," I tell him.

And P.S., I wasn't.

I was talking to myself.

✳ **16** ✳

TOGETHER

"Daddy's home!" Alfie shouts a few hours later.

I have been practicing my two **TEENY-TINY** magic illusions in my room. I'm sick of them, and I know I'm gonna flop tomorrow. But if I have to perform those illusions at the talent show, I might as well do them right.

It's not *their* fault they're small.

Maybe their father tells them that they'll grow bigger any day now.

"Go give him a big hug," Mom tells my little sister. "Why don't you go too, EllRay?" she adds, smiling as if she knows a secret. "Give him a hand with his briefcase, maybe. Or whatever he needs help with. Dinner will be ready in an hour."

So I wander out the kitchen door after Alfie to greet my dad.

He's carrying a white FedEx box under one

arm, which probably means he had something delivered to his office at the college. He claims that things get to San Diego faster than they do to Oak Glen, and he's probably right. San Diego is a big city, and it has an airport.

I like FedEx. Their packages always make things look important.

"EllRay," Dad says, smiling. "Help me out here, would you, son?"

Alfie has wrapped her pudgy golden arms around his legs as part of her big hug. But I think he wants me to take the box he's carrying, not unwrap Alfie from his legs.

I just hope that box isn't full of rocks!

It's not. It's pretty light, in fact.

"Want me to put this in your office?" I ask as Dad hobble-walks to the kitchen door, Alfie still attached to him like a starfish. She likes to walk—and sometimes dance—while standing on his feet.

Being a dad can be hard. On shoes, anyway.

"Good idea," Dad says. "And you can stay in there with it, if you would, while I say hi to your mom and wash my hands," he adds. "I'll be with you

in a minute. *It's a secret*," he mouths, so Alfie can't
hear this last part.

A secret? *What's* a secret?

"First things first," Dad says after he and I have sat down on the small sofa in his office. "Did you talk to Mr. James?"

"Who's Mr. James?" I ask, my heart thudding, because—**UH-OH**. Did I forget some important assignment Mom or Dad gave me?

Oh, my poor aching brain!

"He's been your principal for the past couple of years, EllRay," Dad says in his too-patient voice. "Honestly. I think you have a mental block about some things."

One mental block? I have a whole toy box full of them, Dad!

I nod my head. "I saw him," I report, sighing. "And I told him why I should drop out of the show. And he said he understood, but no way. He said the program was already being printed up with my name on it. And that's just dumb. Like some copy machine is the boss," I say, these last words tumbling out. "Because he could have made an announcement. You know, about how I wasn't going to be in the show."

"I suppose he thinks it's no big deal," Dad says as if he's trying to put himself inside the principal's probably hairy brain. "He must figure that you'll just be onstage for a few minutes, and then it will be over."

"Then *everything* will be over," I say in my gloomiest voice. "Because I'll be a flop, and then my reputation will be ruined forever. Or at least for the next three years. 'EllRay the Magnificent.' Hah!"

"I think that saying your reputation would be ruined is something of an exaggeration, EllRay," my dad says. "But I thought that's what your principal might say. And yet your mother tells me you've been practicing your two illusions all afternoon," he says, looking thoughtful.

"Well, yeah," I say. "I want to try as hard as I can, at least."

Uh-oh. I said "yeah" instead of "yes." But for once, Dad ignores my so-called lazy tongue. "That's excellent," he says, smiling as he brushes the palm of his big hand across the top of my head, the closest he gets to being mushy with me. "But I have a surprise for you, son."

"In the box?" I ask, peeking over at his desk.

"That's right," my dad says. "I did some pretty major research online Tuesday night, after you and I talked, and I found three really good illusions I think you can do. Ones that will work well in a big auditorium. My research took some time, but I hope you'll think the results are worth it."

"You bought me three brand-new magic tricks? Tricks that we didn't make at home, out of string and straws?" I say, forgetting to use the word "illusions" for a second, I'm so excited—and surprised.

Because like I've said before, my dad is thrifty, and that's putting it mildly. "Thrifty" means he doesn't like spending money if he doesn't have to. He likes to *save*—for college for Alfie and me, for retirement, for Christmas.

You name it, he saves for it.

Yet he studied the magic store sites online, when he could have been thinking about his radio isotopes, whatever they are, and then he bought me three probably expensive illusions? Not to mention the extra money he spent for super-fast delivery!

They print the postage cost on the box, and it was so high it made me blink.

This whole thing is just so—so *un-Dad*.

He nods. "I did," he tells me, smiling some more. "I could see how important it was to you, EllRay. And your mother and I thought you should at least have a *chance* at making the splash you want to at the talent show."

"It's not so much about making a splash," I try to explain. "It'll be the big kids who do that, and maybe even Jared and Stanley dancing hip hop. I just want to be able to hold my head up high when it's over. But—but—I can't believe it," I sputter, staring at the white box sitting on Dad's desk. "Three new illusions? What are they?"

There could be anything in that box!

I hope not a magician's live white rabbit, though. There aren't any airholes in FedEx boxes.

"Well, let's open it up and see," Dad says with a laugh. "Because you are now the proud owner of 'The Magic Flower Pot,' son, and 'Color-Changing Scarves,' and 'The Jumbo Change Bag' illusions. And I'll help you figure them all out after dinner. Then you can decide which two of the three you want to perform tomorrow, and I'll help you practice until you're good to go. And I'm going to be in the audience tomorrow afternoon, too—whatever it takes. We're a team, son."

"A team?" I ask, trying out the word as if I've never heard it before.

I kind of like it!

But—me, EllRay Jakes? Forgetter of permission slips, principals' names, seven-times-anything, and library books? And my dad, the brainiac rock scientist college teacher who has never lost a thing in his life except some of his hair? A *team*?

"Never doubt it," my father tells me, his voice suddenly serious. "So go on, EllRay. Bring that bad boy over here, and let's open it up and take a look."

"Together," I say.

I like that word, too!

✳ **17** ✳

AN EXTRA-SPECIAL DAY

It's talent show day!

When a day like your birthday is coming, it comes slow. But when a scary day like today comes, it comes fast. Why is that?

I decided to perform "The Magic Flower Pot" and "The Jumbo Change Bag" illusions, and Dad helped me practice each of them for a long time last night. He was calm but serious, as if he had just discovered some amazing new crystal.

I think it's the longest time my dad and I ever spent together doing a me-thing.

It was so cool.

Still, the thought of doing my new illusions in front of the whole school makes me want to fall over like a tree that just got cut down in the forest. Timber-r-r! *CLUNK*.

But big illusions are sometimes easier than the

smaller ones, we discovered. At least I won't have to try to balance two quarters sideways between my still-very-short fingers.

Should I tell the principal that I'm doing different illusions from the ones I did at the tryouts? I don't think so.

But I probably *will* have to get permission to have someone come up on stage with me. My dad says a magician usually calls this person "my lovely assistant," so I guess it had better be a girl or a woman. But I'm not gonna call her "my lovely assistant," that's for sure.

I mean, *EW*.

"I made you some scrambled eggs," my mom tells me at breakfast, smiling.

"She made some for me, too," Alfie pipes up from the kitchen table.

"I don't think I can eat," I tell Mom, fidgeting with the buttons on the dress-up shirt she ironed for me last night. Why can't I wear a regular T-shirt? It's just kids who are going to see me perform!

And all the teachers, I remind myself, my heart starting to pound. *And* a bunch of parents.

But does Mom really think I'll still look this

sharp by two o'clock this afternoon? She's a dreamer! But I guess I already knew that. That's probably what writers are.

"You have to keep up your strength, EllRay," Mom tells me, giving me a squeeze. "Today's your big day."

"Don't remind me," I beg.

"Today's my big day, too," Alfie says, since she hates being left out of anything. "I'm just as much a person as EllWay, Mom," she continues. "We both come up to *here*, don't we?" she says, patting the top of her head.

Alfie can say these really goofy things and still make sense, in a way. "It's her gift," my dad sometimes tells Mom and me.

"You're right, honeybun," my mom says, laughing. "But each of us gets an extra-special day every so often, and this one is EllRay's. And the rest of us will help celebrate it. That's what families do."

"*Mom*," I say. Can't she change the subject? I choke down a bite or two of scrambled eggs and then mess up the rest so it looks like I've eaten more. I cover what is left with half a piece of toast.

"She means I'm coming to the talent show too,"

Alfie informs me, her mouth full of eggs.

"You *are*? Because it's really not that big a deal," I say.

Alfie at the talent show. Anything could happen!

"And I'm coming to the wedding shower too," Alfie says. "Because Mom is on the committee, and there's gonna be *cake*. With fwosting woses."

Frosting roses.

"Huh," I say.

But the truth is, I don't mind Alfie coming to the talent show *or* the wedding shower. Some kids in my class already know her, and I kind of like showing her off. That's how cute she is. But like I said before, don't tell her.

I just wish the talent show and the party weren't happening on the same day. Why can't life spread things out better? Most days are so *boring*!

"Your dad's giving you his old briefcase for your magic supplies," Mom says as I get up from the table. "It's at the bottom of the stairs. He had to leave early this morning to get some work done, so he could join Alfie and me later on at school."

"Huh," I say again. I think my brain is stuck.

But it'll be pretty cool carrying a briefcase full of magic to school.

If only I didn't have to *do* anything this afternoon.

If only we could cut straight to the cake.

"And now," I hear the principal say into a microphone at two o'clock that afternoon, "I welcome you all on this lovely April day to Oak Glen Primary School's Talent Show."

"*Yay-y-y-y!*" the audience roars, and the performers—who are all backstage—look at each other. Our eyes are wide with either excitement or fright.

I wish Corey and his freckles were here! But he had to leave just after lunch. We will be going by grade, so at least Jared, Stanley, and I won't have to perform after the sixth-graders. Three of the sixth grade girls are already warming up in the shadows. They look like they could be in a music video, only they have more clothes on. Still, try competing with that!

About twelve kindergarten kids are already onstage, behind the closed curtain. They are wearing long, construction paper dog ears that are tied around their heads with yarn. Their teacher and Miss Myrna are struggling to keep them quiet and in two neat rows. "Now, nobody get the yips," I hear Miss Myrna say.

"First," the principal announces to the audience, "I present to you some gifted members of Oak Glen's very own kindergarten class. They will treat us all to their version of 'You Ain't Nothin' but a Hound Dog.' So put those hands together!" he says, and the audience claps their hands.

The music begins, and the little kids start dancing like crazy, flapping their arms and pretending to wag invisible tails. Eleven of them do, anyway. One boy in the back row just stands there frozen, staring out at the audience with horrified eyes. I guess that's "the yips."

I'm with you, kid.

They amble offstage after taking their bows, even the once-frozen boy, who is now smiling like he won a race, and they take their seats in the audience. Most of them are still wearing their construction paper dog ears. They'll probably have them on all weekend. Alfie would.

The first- and second-graders' acts go by pretty fast. First, a couple of tiny girls sing a song from *Lion King* while three boys stomp around, pretending to be wild animals.

Next, in front of the curtain, a few little girls do the hula to loud Hawaiian music. Fake flowers circle their heads the way they do on Alfie's pink plastic horse, though the girls' tucked-in T-shirts and sneakers kind of ruin the effect. As the girls step and sway, and their grass skirts swish, three boys pretend to play plastic ukuleles. One of them is rocking out like he's a finalist at an air guitar contest.

"*Yay-y-y-y!*" everyone in the audience cheers as they curtsy and bow.

And—it's time for the third grade to perform. **I'M UP NEXT**.

✿ **18** ✿

ABRACADABRA, ELLRAY JAKES!

Time is going by very s-l-o-w-l-y now, and there is a roaring sound in my ears.

What if I hurl onstage? Will *that* count as talent, Mr. Principal?

I'd have to move if that happened!

Miss Myrna has set up a table with a white cloth on it behind the curtain. My two new illusions are on it, waiting for me. I even get to use a microphone, but I probably won't remember what I'm supposed to say.

And Mom and Dad and Alfie are somewhere out there in the audience.

At least my dress-up shirt still looks pretty good. I skipped lunch, that's why.

"Now," the principal says, "for your viewing pleasure, ladies and gentlemen, boys and girls, I present a magic act that will astound you. You will have to watch carefully, though, because these tricks are small, so they might be hard to see. But before we begin, I need a volunteer from the audience to assist our young magician."

"Me! Me! Me!" I hear a bunch of little kids yell, but the principal and I have worked this out in advance.

"Who is that I see volunteering?" the principal says, peering out at the audience. "Why, it's our very own Ms. Sanchez!"

"Really?" I hear Ms. Sanchez say from where she is sitting.

And everyone laughs, because they can tell she didn't know her name would be called.

I imagine Ms. Sanchez hurrying up onto the stage and standing next to the principal.

Still hidden by the curtain, I walk onto the center of the stage like I am heading to the principal's office—in trouble and doomed.

Been there. Done that. "Bought the T-shirt," as my dad always adds.

"Without further ado," the principal says, "I give you Oak Glen Primary School's only magician, Ell-Ray Jakes!"

And the curtain parts. Ms. Sanchez walks over to join me, her heels clicking on the scuffed-up stage. She looks extra pretty today, probably because of the party later. She's wearing a yellow dress.

"Good afternoon, and welcome to my world of magic," I boom into the microphone in my deepest, most magical voice, the one my dad helped me find last night.

Ms. Sanchez smiles her encouragement, and I suddenly remember every reason from the past year why I like her so much. I'm gonna *miss* her next year.

"First," I say, "I present to you this completely empty, but very beautiful, bag."

And I pick up the big, bright red magic change bag. It has gold dragons on the outside, and it is black inside, and it has a zipper at the bottom. Long tassels dangle from each end of the zipper. I show the bag to everyone, including Ms. Sanchez, of course.

"It's empty," she announces in a loud, clear voice.

A change bag is made out of silky cloth. It hangs from a wood circle that the magician holds using the long wood handle attached to it. There is a hidden compartment inside the bag which can only be opened by a flat metal switch under the change bag's handle, right next to the bag. But Ms. Sanchez can't see any of this.

"I will now unzip the bottom of this bag," I say, "to show you that it truly is empty. Ms. Sanchez?" I say, swinging the unzipped bag her way again. "Will you please stick your arm through this bag and show the audience how empty it is?"

And her arm goes through the dark inside of the bag and comes straight out the bottom. "Totally empty," she announces, waving hi to the audience while she's at it.

And everyone **LAUGHS**.

Ms. Sanchez pulls her hand out of the bag. I zip it back up.

"But what's this?" I ask everyone, working the metal switches under the handle to open up the hidden compartment. "Why, it's a beautiful scarf!"

And from out of the hidden compartment I pull a long, skinny, rainbow-colored scarf. "*Yay-y-y-y!*" people cheer, and I bow to Ms. Sanchez and hand it to her in a fancy, magical way.

She really looks surprised! She puts her hand

to her chest, staggers back a couple of steps, then recovers. Then she wraps the scarf around her neck a few times like a model in one of my mom's magazines.

I *knew* Ms. Sanchez would be a good "lovely assistant"!

I wish Corey was here to see this.

I put down the change bag, and I pick up an empty plastic flower pot and a magic wand tipped at each end with a golden band. Dad drew a little

X on one band, but I'm the only one who knows it's there.

"And for my final trick," I tell everyone loudly, to quiet the excited conversations that have sprung up, "I present to you this empty flower pot." I pick it up, then rattle my wand around inside the flower pot to show just how empty it is. "Ms. Sanchez?" I say, handing the empty pot to her. She examines it inside and out and nods at the audience, and I take it back.

"But what is this?" I say, putting my magic wand inside the pot, X-side down. I press the tip of the wand down hard against the bottom of the pot, and it latches on tight—because there are really strong magnets hidden in both the pot bottom and the end of the wand. *"Abracadabra!"* I say.

I tug on the wand, and up pops the huge, colorful bunch of feather flowers that were crammed down under the pot's false bottom. "Ta-da!" I say, and I hand the now-blooming flower pot to Ms. Sanchez, who gasps loudly into the microphone, holds out the flower pot up high for everyone to see, then presses her hand to her forehead as if she might faint from astonishment.

And everyone is clapping like crazy! Even the principal, who has never seen these two tricks before.

Somewhere out there, my mom, my dad, and my sister are clapping, too. Alfie's probably telling the person sitting next to her that I'm just faking.

Ms. Sanchez and I bow, and the curtain closes as the audience keeps cheering.

I DID IT. I'm the new King of the Mountain! For a few minutes, anyway.

"That was amazing, EllRay," Ms. Sanchez says, handing me back the scarf and the flower pot as Miss Myrna rolls away my magic table, and Jared and Stanley take the stage. Jared looks like he's about to pass out, and Stanley's hip-hop pants hang so low that they look like they're going to fall off—which would be a big hit with most of the audience. But the principal made him staple them to his shorts, so I know they won't.

"I always knew you were magic, EllRay," Ms. Sanchez says, hugging me tight.

"Thanks," I say, wriggling away. "And thanks for helping me. It was fun."

"For me too, sweetie," Ms. Sanchez says.

And a few kids—even some older ones—high-five and fist-bump me as the principal introduces Jared and Stanley's act.

They changed songs, by the way.

I stumble to my seat in the audience, and the rest of the talent show whizzes by. It includes:

1. Jared and Stanley's hip-hop dance, which is even better than before.

2. A girl doing gymnastics on a mat while a sparkly light ball twirls behind her.

3. Those older fifth-grade girls, all dressed in pink, dancing so hard to the "Barbie Girl" song that the principal starts looking nervous.

4. A bunch of sixth-grade boys dressed up like zombies, doing the old "Thriller" dance.

And those are just the acts I remember.

The Oak Glen Primary School Talent Show *was* fun.

And I got to be part of it!

✻ **19** ✻

WOO-HOO!

"Woo-hoo!" Kevin shouts fifteen minutes later, as he and I barrel into our classroom after school has let out. "Look at all the *food*, dude."

Some third-grade parents were busy decorating the room during the talent show. They put out platters of yummy-looking food, and my stomach growls the second I see it. Lots of little hamburgers and turkey burgers are piled up high, hot dogs have been cut in half—to make eating more of them easier, I guess. And the sandwiches are cut in quarters the fancy way, in triangles. And there's lots of other food, too—including a big bowl of fruit salad, and a huge sheet cake with dozens of roses marching across it like a bunch of frosting soldiers. I have never seen so many roses on a cake.

Everyone will get one, with no fighting. Alfie will be so happy!

I hardly ate a thing today, I was so nervous. Also, like I said, I was trying to keep my shirt clean. But forget that now. Mustard, ketchup, punch, frosting—*bring it on.*

"It's *beautiful*," Annie Pat says, screeching to a stop and clasping her hands as she looks around. "All yellow and white."

"Like a field of flowers," Emma adds, her eyes shining.

Twisted crepe-paper streamers loop all across the ceiling, and flower-bouquetlike bunches of yellow and white helium balloons—helium!—hover in each corner of the room. Maybe we'll each get to bring one home.

And you should see the real flowers. There's pretty music, too—like ice skating music. Alfie is already whirling around in circles.

"Girls line up over here," one of the moms calls out. "We made a little veil for each of you. And boys, you line up over there for your *boutonnieres*."

"What's that?" Jared asks in his most suspicious voice. "Because I am *not* gonna wear a veil, even for cake."

"It's just one little flower you pin to your shirt,"

another mom tells him, laughing. "But you don't need to wear it if you don't want to."

I'll look at it, at least. Flowers are okay. Outside, anyway.

"How do I look?" Kry says, whirling around to face us. A short poufy white veil sprouts from the top of her head.

"Me next," a bunch of girls—including Alfie—are saying, lining up for their veils.

I guess they all get to be pretend brides during this party, at least—which is kind of a scary thought. There aren't as many boys lined up over at the *boutonniere* table, that's for sure.

"EllRay," someone says in a quiet voice.

I turn around, and—Corey's standing there! My best friend! He smells like chlorine, and his freckles look extra speckly, like they're waiting to be counted again.

"You're here," I say, smiling. "What happened to swim practice?"

Corey smiles back at me. "Mom let me leave early when she figured out how much I wanted to come to the party. I don't know what she told my coach. I'll worry about that later. But I missed the talent show," he says, looking sad. "How did it go?"

"Okay," I tell him, trying to be modest.

"EllRay was great, and so were Jared and Stanley," Kevin says, appearing at our sides. "Hey," he says to Corey, grinning like it's old times.

Maybe Kevin *can* be friends with both Jared and me! Even though we're "opposites."

"I'm glad they didn't cut the cake yet," Corey says, looking at the food tables with hungry eyes. A couple of dads—including mine!—are guarding the tables from all the kids who are now in the room. "Not yet, big guy," the other dad says to Jared, who was probably about to dive onto the hamburger platter with his mouth open, like a great white shark.

"Ms. Sanchez and the moms get to go first," my dad tells Jared—and all the other kids, including me, who are eyeing the food as if we haven't eaten in a week.

"And here she is!" a mother exclaims, as Ms. Sanchez enters the room. She looks as pretty as she did onstage.

"Good heavens," she says, her engagement ring hand pressed against her chest. "You girls look adorable," she adds, laughing as she sees all the little veils.

"And here's *your* party veil," Emma's mom says, bringing it over. Emma's mom and my mom pin it carefully to Ms. Sanchez's hair, and our teacher spins around, showing it off to everyone.

"It's not every day a person has a wedding shower," Annie Pat's mother says, her drooly, red-haired baby perched on her hip. "The children really wanted to honor you. They love being in your class so much."

I like it better when people say "kids" instead of "children," but whatever.

"Eat something, Ms. Sanchez," Jared begs. "So we can go next. After the moms, I mean."

"Yeah," Stanley says, like he's seconding a motion. "Please," he adds, catching a look from one of the moms.

"All right, you poor captive children," Ms. Sanchez says with a laugh. She goes to one end of the long food table and takes a plate.

"And the mothers go next," Stanley's plaid shirt–wearing dad reminds us, like he's directing a square dance.

So they line up, too. "I'm little. I'm with her," Alfie announces, pointing up at my mom. Alfie is not about to miss out on any food. **TRUTH**.

Us kids are all keeping an eye on the food platters. We're all worried that there won't be enough— or that the kids who go through the line first will hog everything, and run off cramming hamburgers and hot dogs into their mouths as fast as they can.

But they won't get the chance, because the dads are policing the table. Some of them are even serving up food with long, pinchy tongs.

"Don't worry," my dad calls out. "There's plenty more where this came from!"

And pretty soon, everyone is busy eating and drinking—at *our desks*, which have probably never had so much fun before in their entire lives.

Poor desks!

⚡ **20** ⚡

COUNT ON IT

And that's when Ms. Sanchez's future husband—okay, Mr. Timberlake—enters the room. "Sorry I'm late," he calls out to Ms. Sanchez, who blows a kiss in his direction.

Ew. Mushy. He'd better not kiss her for real.

He heaps his plate high with our food and goes straight to Ms. Sanchez's side.

"It's time for the present," one of the moms announces.

"Hooray!" the parents cheer. A few of them even clap their hands, but not us kids. We know what the present is, so we just keep eating and drinking.

There's ice cream floating in the punch, did I say?

And out from the supply closet comes a big wrapped gift. "For us? What could it be?" Ms. Sanchez asks.

I actually feel sorry for her! I mean, a *vacuum cleaner*? Even if she and her new husband can dance around with it?

But she and Mr. Timberlake look really happy when they open it, which is just sad. I *never* want to grow up if it means that getting a vacuum cleaner is the best thing that happens to you all day. And one present for two people? What's up with that?

"Thanks," they're telling everyone, sounding like they mean it.

"*We* have something for you, too, Ms. Sanchez," Cynthia announces loudly, as if the wedding shower book was all her idea and she didn't keep saying how hard it was going to be to make it. "We did it all by ourselves," Cynthia adds. "Fiona will go get it for you."

And Fiona trots off looking for the cardboard box she brought with her today. She comes back a few seconds later holding a gift-wrapped package with a big, fancy, white-and-silver bow on it. "Here," she says shyly, handing the present to Ms. Sanchez.

"We know nothing about this," one of the moms calls out, holding up her hands to show how innocent the grown-ups are. And they laugh.

"Help me open it?" Ms. Sanchez asks Mr. Timberlake, and together, they tear off the wrapping paper. And there's our book. "*Oh*," Ms. Sanchez exclaims, holding it up for all to see.

Fiona really did great, I think as I stare at the cover. It shows a beautiful bride who looks like a cross between Ms. Sanchez and Barbie, and, as promised, lace ruffles outline the edges of the picture. Glued-down pearls are scattered all around.

Alfie looks like she's about to grab that book and run for the door, it's so pretty.

"I love it," Ms. Sanchez tells us, holding it to her chest and giving Fiona a special look that says without words how much she likes the cover.

"But that's not all," Cynthia says, still in charge. "Because inside, we each wrote what we like about you."

"And we gave you some advice about getting married," Emma adds.

"Oh, boy. This I gotta see," one of the mothers says.

"Maybe someday we'll share it with you," Ms. Sanchez tells the parents. "But we get to read it first. After all, the children made it for us."

For *you*, Ms. Sanchez. For you.

"So let's get on with the party," she says, holding the wedding book tight. She takes a peek inside, and a sunny smile spreads across her face—like the yellow frosting decorating Alfie's golden-brown face.

"We're good for another ten minutes, anyway," Stanley's dad announces. "Because the custodian says we need to start cleaning up pretty soon."

"Aww," a few kids groan. But most of the food is gone, and the presents have been handed over, so why hang around?

"Scrape your plates when you're done, every-one, and then put them in the recycling bag," the recycling mom calls out. I think it's Fiona's mother. She looks a little Fiona-ish. "Punch cups, too," she adds.

"Punch cups, three," Corey says to Kevin and me, being goofy.

"Punch cups, four," Kevin chimes in.

My two best friends are back. For now, anyway. It's magic!

And even though my new illusions are stashed

away in my mom's car, in my new-old briefcase, I suddenly feel like there is magic all over the place. Because apart from my two friends and me being tight again, isn't it also magic that Fiona, the shyest girl in our class, is now standing in the middle of a bunch of admiring kids, all because of the art she made?

And isn't it magic that I turned from a shrimpy, goof-up kid into a magician who didn't hurl or keel over during the all-school talent show?

Me, EllRay Jakes!

And isn't it magic that my dad came through for me the way he did?

MAGIC all over the place!

And it's only April.

I can tell that Ms. Sanchez loves our book. It's her best present by *far*. She's reading even more of it now, in fact, and flashing each of us that special look she gave Fiona a few minutes ago.

Hey, she's walking in my direction! "Hello, there," she says when she reaches me. "A little bird told me that this book was your idea. We can't thank you enough."

We.

"That's okay," I mumble, staring at my sneakers. "I hope you like it. Everybody worked on it," I add, remembering to be fair.

Ms. Sanchez sinks down, pins a daisy *boutonniere* to my good shirt, then puts her arm around my shoulder. She gives it a squeeze. "I'll remember you forever, Mr. EllRay Jakes," she says, speaking softly into my embarrassed ear. "I'm glad we have more time together before we have to say good-bye. Who knows what fun our class will still have? But when the time finally comes, remember that I'll always be here for you—just down the hall from wherever you are. Or someone like me will be down that hall, if they're lucky."

"Really?" I say, looking up into her sparkly brown eyes.

"Really," she promises. "You can count on it."

"Well, okay, then," I say, trying to make a joke out of it. "I guess you can go ahead and marry that guy."

"Thanks, sweetie," she whispers, giving me another hug.

She calls me "sweetie" sometimes. I'm just now getting used to it.

Ms. Sanchez stands up, straightens her skirt, and goes off to talk to somebody else.

But that's all right, because no one can ever take this day away from me.

ABRACADABRA!